Behind the Door

Books by Giorgio Bassani

The Smell of Hay

Behind the Door

Five Stories of Ferrara

The Heron

The Garden of the Finzi-Continis

Giorgio Bassani

Behind
the Door

Translated by William Weaver

Harbrace Paperbound Library

A Helen and Kurt Wolff Book

Harcourt Brace Jovanovich
New York and London

Printed in the United States of America

Library of Congress Cataloging in Publication Data

Bassani, Giorgio.
    Behind the door.

    (Harbrace paperbound library ; HPL 66)
    Translation of Dietro la porta.
    "A Helen and Kurt Wolff book."
    I. Title.
PZ4.B3176Be4   [PQ4807A79]   853'.9'14   75-29308
ISBN 0-15-611685-5

First Harbrace Paperbound Library edition 1976

A B C D E F G H I J

Behind the Door

I

I have been unhappy many times in my life, as a child, as a youth, as a grown man; many times, if I think back, I have touched what are called the depths of despair. And yet I remember few periods darker, for me, than my schooldays in the months between October of 1929 and June of 1930, my first year of Liceo.* The years that have passed since then have been, after all, useless: I have never managed to heal a sorrow that has remained there, intact, like a secret wound, secretly bleeding. Cure myself? Rid myself of it? I know this is impossible. If I write about it now, therefore, it is only in the hope of understanding and of making others understand. That is all I seek.

I felt ill at ease from the very beginning, completely disoriented. I didn't like the classroom to which we had been assigned, at the end of a grim corridor, far from the gay, familiar corridor into which opened the thirteen doors of the Ginnasio classes, the lower grades divided into the three sections and the upper into two. I didn't like the new teachers, with their ironic, detached man-

---

* In the period of this story, the Italian school system comprised five years of elementary school, five years of Ginnasio, and three years of Liceo.

ner, which discouraged any intimacy, any personal consideration (they addressed us with the formal "Lei"), even if they didn't all suggest the regime of prison harshness and severity we could expect from the Greek and Latin professor, Guzzo, and from Signorina Krauss, who taught chemistry and natural sciences. I didn't like my new classmates, who came from the A section of the fifth year of the Ginnasio, to which we of the B section had been united. They were very different from us, it seemed to me—brighter perhaps, better-looking, generally from grander families than ours: ineluctably alien, in other words. And I couldn't understand or excuse, on this score, the behavior of many of *us*, who, unlike me, had immediately tried to make friends with *them*, rewarded —as I saw in alarm—with the same friendliness and with similarly casual acceptance. "How can this be?" I asked myself, unhappy and jealous. "How can it be?" My loyalty, cruelly offended from the very first day of school, when I had glimpsed in the distance my beloved Professor Meldolesi, our literature teacher in the Fifth, disappear at the head of his new fourth-year section along the Ginnasio corridor (a forbidden corridor now, where we would never set foot again), my absurd loyalty demanded that an invisible line of demarcation continue to separate, even in the Liceo, the survivors of the old Fifth sections, so that we from B would be protected and guaranteed forever against all betrayal, all contamination.

But the circumstance that embittered me the most was this: Otello Forti, who had shared a desk with me since elementary school, had not passed, as I had, the final examinations (I myself had had to take a make-up examination in mathematics in October, but he, though

4

he had failed only English, was definitively eliminated after the second try in October). So now he was no longer beside me, seated as always at my right, and I couldn't even meet him outside, when we were let out at noon, to go down Corso Giovecca together, each heading for his own home, or in the afternoon, at the Montagnone, to play football, or at his house especially, his great, beautiful, friendly house, filled with brothers and sisters, girl- and boy-cousins, where I had spent so much of my adolescence. Otello, poor thing, unable to bear the grief of his unjust failure, had asked—and received—his father's permission to go and repeat the Fifth at Padua, in a boarding school run by the Barnabite Fathers. So I was without Otello, unable to sense, at my side, the massive, slightly obtuse presence of his body, so much bigger and heavier than mine, no longer stimulated, or perhaps irritated, by the rough, ironic, but affectionate reserve he adopted toward me sometimes, when, at my house or his, we did our homework together. From the beginning I had felt the persistent grief, the irreparable sense of emptiness that widowers feel. What did it matter that he wrote me letters in which with surprising eloquence (I had never considered him very intelligent) he poured out all his affection? I was now in the Liceo, he was in the Ginnasio. I was in Ferrara; he, in Padua: this was the insuperable reality which he, with the courage, clarity, and sudden maturity of the defeated, realized even more than I did. I wrote to him: "We'll see each other at Christmas." To which he replied yes, at Christmas, in two and a half months, we would probably meet (on condition, however, as he had vowed to himself, that he passed all his subjects: a far from sure eventuality!), but, in any

5

case, ten days spent together wouldn't change the situation. He seemed to be suggesting: "Forget me, go ahead, find another friend—if you haven't already found him." No, writing each other was of little use. And in fact, after the holidays at the beginning of November, All Saints, All Souls, Armistice Day, by tacit agreement we stopped.

I needed to release my discontent, show it. So, on the first day of school, I had taken care not to participate in the usual grab for the best places (those nearest the teacher's desk, that is), on which, as at every year's beginning, my classmates had flung themselves. I had let the others, *us* and *them*, have their way, while I stood at the door to observe the scene with disgust, then finally took a seat in the back, at the last desk of the row reserved for the girls, next to the window in the corner. It was the only vacant place: a large desk, hardly suited to my slight frame, but completely suited, on the other hand, to my intense desire for exile. How many loutish failures, repeaters, it must have seen before me, I said to myself. I read what had been carved deeply in the varnish of the sloping top by the penknives of my predecessors (mostly invectives against the teaching staff and especially against the Principal, Turolla, nicknamed "Half-Pint"), and then as I looked around, toward the thirty-odd necks neatly lined up before me, my eyes— I sensed—became charged with acrimony. My recent failure in mathematics still rankled, true; I couldn't wait to regain ground, to be considered again one of the brightest, the most intelligent. And yet, for the first time in my life, I understood the attitude of the idlers in the back row. The school seen as prison, the Principal as its warden, the professors as turnkeys, and one's classmates

6

as jailbirds: a system not to be accepted in zealous collaboration, but to sabotage and denigrate at every opportunity. Those currents of anarchical contempt which, from elementary days, I had always felt, with fear, wafting from the back of the classrooms—how I understood them, now!

I looked ahead of me, and I disapproved: everything and everybody. The girls, humiliated in their black smocks, as women were no good at all. Tiny, the four at the first two desks (all from the A section of the Fifth), with their lank braids hanging over their skinny backs, looked like tots in kindergarten. What were their names? All ended with *ini:* Bergamini, Bolognini, Santini, Scanavini, Zaccarini: something of the sort, which called up, through an association of similar sounds, petty bourgeois families of tradesmen, grocers, artisans, government employees, cattle dealers, and so on. The two at the third desk, Cavicchi and Gabrieli, the former very fat, the latter tall and skinny with a colorless, pimply face, an old maid of thirteen, were what was left of the ten "females" of Five B: the two ugliest, no doubt, two sexless drudges destined to become pharmacists or schoolteachers, now to be considered mere objects, things. The remaining three, at the fourth and fifth desks, Balboni and Jovine at the fourth, and Manoja, alone, at the fifth, came from out of town: Balboni from the country (and you could tell from the way she was dressed, poor thing; her mother, like as not, was the village dressmaker and had made the daughter's clothes . . .), Jovine was from Potenza, and Manoja from Viterbo: these last two, no doubt, in the wake of police or railway officials, transferred to Northern Italy for special merits. How boring,

7

and how sad! Did all girls who wanted to go on with their studies have to be like this? Dejected bigots, without character (they didn't even wash very frequently, the mummies, to judge by the stale odor they gave off), while beauties like Legnani and Bertoni, for example, the two vamps of Five B, were always failed pitilessly? But they didn't give a damn, Legnani and Bertoni: the first was about to get married—so we heard—and the second, with her wasp waist, her black shiny bangs, and her malicious eyes like the movie star Elsa Merlini's, would hardly sit through the Fifth again. She was the sort to slip off to Rome and become an actress—as we had heard her declare many a time—instead of staying there to gather mold behind the door of the Liceo!

But it was the males who bore the brunt of my criticism, especially the pairs who occupied the desks in the middle row, the one opposite the teacher's dais. Up there, in the first desk and in the second, Five A had situated three of its group, Boldini, Grassi, and Droghetti, and Florestano Donadio, from B section, who sat with Droghetti at the second desk, looked like a tolerated guest, wretched as he was in every way, in his studies, his physique, in everything. Droghetti, son of a cavalry officer, with that foolish and impeccable appearance of his, which, you could count on it, destined him to follow in his father's footsteps, was a mediocrity, to be sure. But the two in front, Boldini and Grassi, among the brightest of Five A, when put together represented real power, to which Donadio, like the scared bird he had always been, blond and pink and tiny, obviously offered himself as vassal. At the third desk, another ill-assorted pair: Giovannini from Five B, and Camurri from A. Not that Giovannini was less bright than the other, mind you; on the contrary, despite his peasant background, our good Walter even managed to express himself in proper Italian. But Gamurri was a gentleman: ugly, nearsighted, ass-licker, but a gentleman. His family (the Camurris who lived on Via Carlo Mayr: who didn't know them?) was among the richest in the city. They owned hundreds of acres out toward Codigoro, in the very area Walter came from, so it wasn't impossible that his father or his grandfather had once been, or might still be, in the service of the Camurri family. . . . At the fourth desk then, alone for some reason, perhaps because nobody had sufficient prestige to sit beside him, there was Cattolica, Carlo Cattolica, who from the first year of Ginnasio had been the undisputed champion of section A (he regularly got eight or nine in all his subjects). It wasn't obvious; but through Camurri and Droghetti, trustworthy backs, bent in front of him, it would be a joke, if need arose, for Cattolica to establish contact with the no less trustworthy Boldini and Grassi at the first desk. This would be seen in Greek and Latin tests, and seen often! Information would be passed from the fourth desk to the first, and vice versa, with the same ease as if *they* had a field telephone at their disposal.

Behind Cattolica, two of *ours:* Mazzanti and Malagù (ours after a manner of speaking, however, since they had joined our ranks only a year ago, after having first failed to pass the so-called "*pons asinorum*"); two blanks, or almost. And then, on my right, bent over the desk solely in self-protection, avoiding as far as possible the investigating eyes of Professor Guzzo especially, were Veronesi and Danieli, the former at least

twenty years old, and the latter even older, ancient was-
trels no good even at sports, and experts in only one subject: all the brothels of the city, from the most expensive
to the cheapest, which they boasted of having visited constantly for years. And even if the places in the row of
desks nearest the door, the one opposite the blackboard,
were parceled out a bit better (at the second desk, Giorgio Selmi had ended up with Chieregatti; at the third,
Ballerini had managed once again to sit with the in-
separable Giovanardi), how could I have resigned myself to pairing off at the fourth desk with Lattuga, abject
and smelly, avoided by all, the scorned Aldo Lattuga,
who only rarely, during Ginnasio, had found somebody
willing to sit next to him, and again this year, like Cattolica, though for diametrically opposed reasons, had remained all alone? No, no, I repeated to myself, better the
solitude of the place I had taken, at the end of the girls'
row. Professor Bianchi, the Italian teacher, had begun the
lesson by reciting a canzone of Dante, and one verse of
it had struck me deeply. It went: "The exile that has
been given me I cherish as an honor." This could be my
device, I thought, my motto.

One day I was idly looking through the panes of the
big window on my left at the sad yard, inhabited by
ravenous cats, which separated the Guarini School building, a former convent, from the flank of the Church of
the Gesù. I thought that it would be pleasant if Giorgio
Selmi, for example, whom I had always liked, after all,
had taken the initiative, on the first day of school, and
had asked me to pair off with him. Both of Selmi's parents were dead. He and his brother Luigi lived with a
paternal uncle, Armando, a lawyer, a sour bachelor of

about sixty, who couldn't wait to be rid of his nephews, sticking one in the Military Academy at Modena and the other in the Naval Academy at Leghorn. Now, why on earth had Giorgio preferred to sit with that grim hack Chieregatti, instead of with me? His uncle's apartment, on Piazza Sacrati (a lawyer's office with a few rooms attached, in which they lived), was surely not very well suited to inviting a friend to come and study together, if it was true, as it seemed to be, that Giorgio studied in his bedroom, a kind of closet, nine feet by twelve. But at my house, on the contrary, there was all the necessary space. The room where I studied was big enough for me, him, and anybody else who might like to join the two of us. My mother, besides, delighted that I now spent my afternoons at home, and not, as in my Ginnasio years, at the Fortis', would certainly prepare splendid snacks with tea, butter, and jam at five o'clock! It was a shame, really, that Giorgio Selmi hadn't sat with me. Envy, jealousy: this was the only reason that could have held him back. My house was too beautiful, too comfortable compared to his. And then I had a mother, while he didn't, he had only a grumpy old uncle. Anti-Semitism, for once, had nothing to do with it; absolutely nothing.

"Psss!"

A faint whistle, from my right, made me start. I wheeled around. It was Veronesi. Crouched behind Mazzanti's back, he was urging me with his thin index finger, incredibly tobacco-stained, to look to the front. What was I doing? he seemed to be saying, half amused, half concerned. What had come over me, fool and madman that I was?

I obeyed. In the absolute silence, flawed only by

some subdued laughter, the whole class was looking at me. And so was Professor Guzzo, up there, seated at his desk, staring at me and sneering.

"At last," he said, in a dulcet tone.

I stood up.

"What's your name?"

In a weak voice, I stammered out my name.

Guzzo was famous for being sarcastic, a sarcasm that bordered on sadism. Approaching fifty, tall, Herculean, with large, lizard-colored eyes flashing below a vast brow, like Wagner's, and long gray sideburns that came halfway down his bony cheeks, he was considered at the Guarini a kind of genius (*"Mors domuit corpora— Vicit mortem virtus"*: he had composed the epigraph on the Monument to the Dead in the 1915–18 war). He didn't have a Fascist party card; and for this reason— and only for this reason—he was unable to achieve that university chair to which some philological writings of his, published in Germany, surely entitled him.

"What?" he asked, putting his hand behind his ear and leaning forward so that his broad chest rested on the open ledger. "Raise your voice, please!"

He was enjoying himself, obviously; he was playing.

I repeated my name.

He sat erect brusquely, checked the ledger with care.

"Very well," he concluded, as he made a mysterious mark in the book with his pen.

"And now tell me a bit about yourself," he went on, resting his back against the chair once more.

"About me?"

"Yes, of course, about you. Which section of the Fifth were you in? A or B?"

"B."

He grimaced.

"Ah, B. Good. And how did you arrive here? All at once, at first flight (forgive my lack of memory), or, tell me, was it at a second try?"

"I had to make up mathematics in October."

"Only mathematics."

I nodded.

"Are you sure you didn't have to *make up* (unfortunate, though effective, expression) some other subject as well? Greek and Latin, for example?"

I denied the charge.

"Are you really sure?" he insisted, with feline gentleness.

I denied again.

"Well then, pay attention, my dear young man, pay close attention. . . . I would be sorry if, in addition to mathematics, next summer you were obliged also to make up *Latin and Greek*, but . . . *quod Deus avertat* . . . three subjects . . . You grasp my meaning, don't you?"

He then asked me how I had got along in Ginnasio, and if I had ever had to repeat a year. But he wasn't looking at me: his eyes moved around the room, as if he didn't trust me and were calling for the testimony of some volunteer witness.

"He's very good. One of the best," somebody dared say, perhaps Pavani, in the first desk of the first row.

"Ah, one of the best!" Professor Guzzo cried. "Now then, if in Ginnasio he *was* really one of the best, what is the cause of this decline? How did it happen?"

I didn't know what to say. I stared at my desk as if

the answer Guzzo wanted could come to me from that old, blackened wood. I looked up again.

"How is it?" he went on, implacably. "And why did you choose such a desk? Perhaps so as to be near the excellent Veronesi and the no less excellent Danieli . . . so as to learn from them, rather than from me, *true* Wisdom?"

The class burst into unanimous laughter. Even Veronesi and Danieli laughed, though with less enthusiasm.

"No, no, believe me," Guzzo went on, dominating the tumult with a broad, conductor's gesture. "First of all, you must change your place."

He looked around, examined and evaluated the situation.

"There. At the fourth desk. Next to that gentleman there."

He was pointing to Cattolica.

"What's your name?"

Cattolica rose to his feet.

"Carlo Cattolica," he answered, simply.

"Ah, very good . . . the *celebrated* Cattolica . . . very good. You come from Five A, don't you?"

"Yes, sir."

"Very good. A with B. Excellent."

I collected my books, stepped into the side aisle, reached my new desk, hailed, as I passed, by a little farewell cough from Veronesi, and a welcoming smile from the champion of section A.

"Mind you, Cattolica," Guzzo said meanwhile, "I'm entrusting him to you. Lead this straying sheep back to the straight and narrow path."

II

I don't know what became of Carlo Cattolica, in later life.

He is one of my few schoolmates about whom I know nothing: what sort of career he had, if he married, where he lives, if he is living. I can only say that in 1933, after he had brilliantly passed his final examinations, his family moved: to Turin, I think, where his father, an engineer (a little bald man with blue eyes, slightly mad: a passionate operagoer and stamp collector, completely dominated by a sergeant-major of a wife, who taught mathematics and was a full head taller than he), had unthinkably found a position at the Fiat plant. Did he, Cattolica junior, then become a surgeon as, in Liceo days, self-confident as usual, he had already announced he would be? Did he actually marry the girl he went to see every evening at Bondeno, with his bicycle, and to whom he had been "officially" engaged then for more than a year (Accolti, I think her name was, Graziella Accolti)? Our generation was mistreated like few others; the war and the rest overwhelmed, among our number, many determinations and vocations as firm as Carlo Cattolica's. And yet, God knows why, something tells me that the account between me and my desk-mate in the first year of Liceo is not closed. I am sure that he is alive, that he is a surgeon as he dreamed (if not famous, he must be close to fame), and that, after at least ten years of engagement, he also married his Graziella. His face and Luciano Pulga's are two that, someday, I don't know how, I will come upon again. I feel it, and I expect it.

I can still see Cattolica's face with its sharp profile, etched at my right with exquisite precision, with a medal's sharpness. He was tall, very thin, with burning black eyes, deep, beneath arched, rather protruding brows, and a forehead which was not high, but broad, pale, calm, very handsome. It's odd, but the most distant memory I have of him is also in profile. We went to the same elementary school, the Alfonso Varano on Via Bellaria, but were in different sections even then; and one morning, in the courtyard of the school, during recreation, I was struck by his way of running. He sped along the wall of the yard moving his slim legs with a broad, regular stride like a real middle-distance runner. I asked Otello Forti who he was. "What? Don't you know him? That's Cattolica!" he answered, amazed. He ran, I saw, in a way absolutely different from all the others, including me, who could be distracted or diverted by any trifle. He ran on, looking calmly straight ahead, as if he alone, among so many, knew exactly where he was going.

We were sitting, now, a few inches from each other, but something, a kind of barrier invisible to the naked eye, a secret boundary line, prevented us from communicating with the easy familiarity of friendship. To tell the truth, at first I did attempt some timid approaches: for example, one day when we had written work to do in Latin class, I asked if, this once, I could place my two

16

heavy volumes of Georges beyond the little partition which divided the space for books and papers into two rigorously equal parts. But the cold turning of his face with which Cattolica consented promptly dissuaded me from going on with other maneuvers of this kind. Like a bridal pair, united not through spontaneous choice but by a superior will, we were together, both well aware of the social significance and the worldly importance of our union. He, Cattolica, in Ginnasio, had always been the brightest in section A: from the first year through the fifth (not to mention the elementary grades when the teachers passed his compositions around among themselves, in the corridors). But I, too, with an occasional lapse (mathematics had always been my weak spot, true; but what does mathematics count in the classical department of Liceo?), I, too, after all, had always belonged to the limited group of leaders. . . . Polite, well-mannered, yes; even ready to pretend, in front of the others, the affection and solidarity of better-paired couples; but basically aliens, covert rivals, indeed enemies. And wasn't it right, after all?, I thought, wasn't it proper that, since we were the standard bearers of the two opposing squads, *ab antiquo*, we should behave like this? Each in his place: wasn't this the rule I had wanted everybody to follow?

Normally we made a great show of consideration for each other, the maximum respect and courtesy. Coming back to the desk, for example, after being questioned, we were always generous with reciprocal smiles of approval or consolation, congratulatory or comradely handshakes, even worried about Mazzanti, behind us, who, aware of the situation and alert to the possibility of exploiting it in some way for his own and Malagù's benefit, had immediately started keeping a private ledger where, day after day, he carefully put down all our marks. We were afraid he would give one of our marks to the other, he might not be the impartial judge, the devoted, pedestrian scorekeeper he professed to be. But then, during written work, the fragile castles of social hypocrisy dissolved like mist in the sun, brutally. Then no passage of Greek or Latin was difficult enough to induce us to join our efforts in order to solve it. Each worked on his own, jealous of his personal results, sordidly selfish, ready perhaps to turn in an incomplete or mistaken paper rather than owe the other something. As I had foreseen, Droghetti and Camurri, one behind the other, acted, in front of us, as faithful relays between Cattolica and the distant outposts Boldini and Grassi. When time was pressing, when Professor Guzzo, raising his eyes from the proofs of his essay on Suetonius, announced with a cruel smile that in exactly ten minutes, and not a second more, he was going to send around the "excellent" Chieregatti to collect "the achievements of the ladies and gentlemen present," then the telephone network of section A was something to be seen, as it went into action with shameless perfection! At those crises, our smiles and handshakes were forgotten, our pretended display of comradely courtesy. The mask was off. And once it was off, Cattolica's irreproachable face, overcome by partisan agitation, was displayed to me in all its hostile, odious reality. Naked, at last.

And yet, though I loathed him, I admired and envied him.

Perfect in everything: in Italian as in Latin, in Greek

as in history and philosophy, in science as in mathematics and physics, art history and even gymnastics (I was excused from religion, and did not attend Father Galeassi's lessons; but I was sure that also with the priest Cattolica was impeccable), I hated and also envied the clarity of his mind, the lucid working of his brain. What a muddled bungler I was, compared to him! But not always, anyway, because there were themes and themes: some I liked, others not, and when a subject didn't appeal to me there was nothing to be done, I was lucky if I could get a six. And so I shone more perhaps in the oral tests in Latin and Greek (after our initial skirmish, Guzzo had taken a liking to me; when we were reading Homer or Herodotus—especially Herodotus—he almost always called on me to have, as he said, "the precise translation"), but in written tests, especially in translating Italian into Latin, Cattolica was distinctly my better: he remembered all the most recondite rules of morphology and syntax, and, in practice, he never made a mistake. His memory allowed him, when we were questioned in history, to fire off a list of dozens and dozens of dates, without missing one, and when it came to natural sciences he could reel off the classifications of the Invertebrates, to the ecstatic Signorina Krauss, with the same confidence and nonchalance as if he were reading them from a book. My God, how did he do it? I asked myself. What was hidden in his skull? An adding machine? Mazzanti, for his part, never hesitated: after such demonstrations of mnemonic efficiency, he was ready to mark a nine, even a nine plus in his private ledger. And the funny thing is that the "plus" was often added because I turned in my seat and insisted on it.

But my sense of inferiority was not inspired so much by the comparison of our respective scholastic attainments as by all the rest.

In the first place, height. He was tall, thin, already a young man, and he dressed like a young man, with long gray flannel trousers, "odd" jackets of heavy tweed, a ten-pack of Macedonias in his pocket, and a handsome silk ascot around his neck; while I, short and stocky as I was, afflicted by the eternal knickers that my mother adored, what could I seem, beside him, except a child? And then: sports. Cattolica engaged in none, he scorned football, and not because he didn't know how to play (once, in front of the Gesù, he had kicked the ball around a bit, showing an excellent style), but just because sports didn't interest him, he considered them a waste of time. Besides, what would I major in at the university? I didn't know: one day I leaned toward medicine, another toward law, another toward literature; whereas he, on the contrary, had not only chosen medicine but had even decided, between internal medicine and surgery, on the latter. And there was finally the girl with whom he made love, the girl at Bondeno. When it came to "girl friends" I still hadn't the slightest real, concrete experience (could you consider experiences what I had had at the sea, in summer, with the little girls on the beach? Some hand-holding, long looks, furtive kisses on the cheek, and no more . . .), whereas he, the only one, I believe, in the whole Liceo, was actually engaged: with parents' consent, and with a ring on his finger. Oh, that ring! It was a sapphire in a white-gold setting, an important ring, a Commendatore's ornament, particularly hateful. And yet how I would have liked to own one too! Who knows?

I said to myself. Perhaps, to become a man, or at least to gain that minimum self-confidence indispensable to passing for a man, such a ring was right, it could be a great help.

With whom did he do his homework, Cattolica, in the afternoon? At the beginning I hadn't realized. He seemed so self-sufficient, so unreachable, that I inclined to believe he had no true, personal friend. I thought even his relations with Boldini and Grassi were purely an emergency matter, and at his house on Via Cittadella no classmate was ever received, not even they.

But I was mistaken.

To tell the truth, I had sensed something even before: that morning when I had been the last to go down the steps from the chemistry and natural sciences laboratory (the undisputed realm of la Krauss), and there, raising my eyes, suddenly I found the three of them in front of me—Cattolica, Boldini, and Grassi—on a landing, talking together. The moment I glimpsed them, I guessed they were arranging to meet that afternoon, in one of their houses. In fact, when they saw me coming, they immediately changed the subject. They plunged into a discussion of football, imagine! As if I didn't know that Cattolica cared nothing for sport and never talked about it.

Still I wanted to see, to make sure. And so, that same afternoon, not having found my father at the Merchants Club (since I no longer studied with Otello, I used to go by on my bicycle and meet him almost every evening, around seven), suddenly I made up my mind: instead of going directly home, I hurried and lay in wait at the corner of Viale Cavour and Via Cittadella.

It was about twenty to eight. From the Castle to the Customs Gate, Viale Cavour was gleaming with lights, while Via Cittadella, broad and stony, seemed immersed in a kind of dark fog. Standing at the corner, I stared at the Cattolica house, about a hundred yards away. It was a little reddish, three-story building, recently constructed and all alone: attractive, to be sure, I said to myself, but with something vaguely vulgar about it. Those curtains that hung at the lighted windows of the third floor, for example: weren't they vulgar, not to say shady? The Pensione Franca and the Pensione Mafarka, on Via Colomba, where Danieli and Veronesi were regular visitors, allowed a glimpse of similar curtains, beyond the half-closed shutters.

A quarter of an hour went by. And I was already preparing to leave (in the end I began to suspect they had met elsewhere, at Grassi's house on Piazza Ariostea or at Boldini's on Via Ripagrande) when the door opened, and, one after another, all three came out, Cattolica included.

On their bicycles, the three came up Via Cittadella to Viale Cavour; luckily, they came slowly enough to give me time to jump onto my bike and move about fifty yards away from the corner. When they reached it, they separated: Boldini and Grassi turned left, toward the center of the city; Cattolica, to the right, toward the Customs Gate.

Where was Cattolica going now? To his girl, at Bondeno? Or merely to the station, to mail a letter, or, who knows, to meet somebody arriving? The idea that he, after a day of hard study (the morning at school, surrounded by general respect, the afternoon at home, sup-

22

ported by the homage and affection of his dearest friends), could also grant himself the luxury of having supper at his fiancée's house seemed unbearable to me.

I followed him at a distance, my eyes on the intensely red little taillight of his bike. He pedaled calmly, as usual without turning around, content and sure of himself and of the gleaming gray Majno which he was riding, supplied with every sort of accessory, as he went to the girl who loved him and was expecting him.

But was his fiancée really expecting him?

She was. When he reached the gate, Cattolica turned left, in fact, down the road toward Bondeno. And now that I was certain how things stood (it was late, too, after eight thirty), now I could give up a pursuit that had become superfluous and let him go.

III

Though Otello Forti received an excellent report at the end of the first term, he didn't want to spend more than three days with his family: Christmas Eve, Christmas, and the day after. So I barely caught a glimpse of him, the afternoon of the 26th, a few hours before he left for Padua, and was already completely involved in his departure.

I went to see him at his house, number 24 Via Montebello.

He took me at once to admire the great, resplendent crèche, set up, as always, in the living room on the ground floor (in that same room, since his parents' death, Otello has installed his dentist's office). That year, for the first time in at least ten years, none of his brothers had remembered to invite me to help arrange it. Then we went up to his room. But not even there, on the top floor, in that little room I had always considered a bit mine, not even there could I make myself useful. Once we were inside, Otello, with strange politeness, had me sit in the armchair by the window. Then he started packing his suitcase. And when I got up from the chair to help him, he insisted I sit down again. He preferred to do it by himself, he said; he would manage much faster alone.

At his insistence, I obeyed. I went and sat in the chair again and, meanwhile, I watched him. He fidgeted over the suitcase with a slowness that seemed studied to me, and he never looked up. I remembered him blonder, fatter, pinker; and perhaps, apart from the long trousers which did make him thinner, perhaps he really had lost weight and grown an inch or so. But in his eyes especially, behind his thick glasses, there was now a serious, grave, bitter expression which saddened and wounded me. It was true, I thought, he had never had a very outgoing disposition. Of the two of us, I had always been the one to take the initiative in everything, in our games, in our bicycle excursions into the country, in our extracurricular reading (Salgari, Verne, Dumas); he, for his part, had allowed himself to be led, grumbling and recalcitrant, but occasionally even laughing, thank God, and secretly admiring me, I felt, precisely because I succeeded in the difficult enterprise of making him laugh from time to time. But now? What had changed us? What fault was it of mine, if he had failed? Why didn't he drop that glumness?

"What's wrong with you?" I tried asking him.

"Me? Nothing. Why?"

"Oh, I don't know. You almost seem angry with me."

"You're lucky: you never change," he answered, with a brief smile that didn't go beyond his lips.

He was referring, obviously, to my inveterate tendency to become upset over trifles, my eternal need for

25

others to be fond of me; and, at the same time, to the change that adversity had wrought in his character. If I felt like it, I could go on amusing myself with my usual stupid childish caprices. But not he: he no longer had the time or the desire. Adversity had made a man of him; and a man has to stick to hard facts.

"I don't know what you mean," I answered. "But really, is this any way to behave? If you had written, at least . . ."

"I believe I did write you. Didn't you get my letters?"

"Yes, of course, but . . ."

"Well, then!"

He raised his eyes and looked at me: harsh, hostile.

"How many times did you write me? Three letters in the first two weeks, then nothing."

"What about you?"

He was right; I had been the first not to answer. But how could I explain to him, now, the reasons why I hadn't felt like keeping up a correspondence in which the roles, between us, had been rudely reversed? I had thought it my task to console him for his bad luck. And instead, he had been the one somehow, from the beginning, to console and admonish.

Later, since it was such a mild day (there was no comparison with the severe winter of the year before; despite the late season, the great cold hadn't yet made up its mind to arrive), we went down to stroll in the garden. In the blue, faintly misty twilight air we made a kind of general reconnaissance of the places dear to our friendship: the handsome central lawn, now damp and bare, where he and I, with his brothers and cousins, had played so many games of croquet; the rustic hut, beyond the lawn, whose ground floor served as a bin for coal and wood, and its upper floor as a dovecote; and finally, the little wooded hillock, near the far wall, where Giuseppe, Otello's elder brother, had set up his personal rabbit hutch, breeding them in a brown shed, half worm-eaten planks and half fencing, a former chicken coop. Now Otello was the one who did most of the talking. He told me at some length about his life in the boarding school: hard, to be sure, he admitted, chiefly because of the impossible hour at which the "prefects" forced them to get up in the morning (they had to wake at five thirty, and then all down to the chapel, to pray), but it was "well worked out," because you were never idle, you always had something to keep you busy. The curriculum? Much more comprehensive than what we had studied last year. In Latin he was working on the third book of the *Aeneid*, Cicero's letters, Sallust's *Jugurthine War*; in Greek, Xenophon's *Cyropaedia*, Lucian's *Dialogues*, and a selection from Plutarch's *Parallel Lives*; in Italian, *I promessi sposi* and *Orlando furioso*.

"All of *Orlando furioso*?" I exclaimed, amazed.

"Yes, all of it," he answered curtly.

But there was one question I was burning to ask him, and I brought myself to ask it only at the end, in the doorway, as I was about to leave.

I asked him: "Have you made friends with anybody?"

To which he replied, with obvious satisfaction, yes, of course, he had met a very nice boy from Venice, and they studied together. His name was Alverà, Leonardo Alverà (his father was a Count!); "also" very bright in

Italian, Latin, and Greek, but especially in mathematics and geometry, subjects in which he was absolutely unbeatable. Did I still scribble a poem every now and then, or a story? Well, Leonardo, with the same ease, solved complicated third-degree equations for his own pleasure. He was a wonder! With a head like his, he would probably become a scientist when he grew up, an inventor, a celebrity, in other words . . .

I can't state with certainty whether what I am now about to tell really happened on the morning of January 8th, the reopening of school after the Epiphany; but I think it did, and in any case I will write it now, before I forget. The fact is that one morning (perhaps a bit before Christmas, but perhaps afterward, just after the holidays; anyway, it was early in the morning, half an hour before the bell) I went into the Gesù. (I had never set foot in that church. Every time Otello went in, because of a test or an important examination in class, "to propitiate the Gods"—so I thought to myself, pitying him—I had simply accompanied him to the threshold, without crossing it.)

That morning, certainly because of the hour, the church was deserted. I walked slowly down the right nave, my nose in the air like a tourist; but the sunlight, falling through the broad upper windows, prevented me from seeing clearly the great baroque canvases over the altars. When I reached the transept, immersed in semidarkness, I moved to the left nave, which was plunged in light. But here my attention was immediately drawn to a kind of strange gathering of people, immobile and silent, in a group beside the second of the two smaller entrances.

Who were they? As I was able to realize as soon as,

almost running, I had come within a certain distance, they were not living people. They were statues: painted wooden statues, life-sized. And they were, in fact, the famous *Pianzún d'la Rosa*, to which, as a child, I had been led many times by Aunt Malvina (the only Catholic aunt I had), not there, however, in the Gesù, but in the Chiesa della Rosa on Via Armari, from which they had evidently been moved later. I looked once more at the atrocious scene: the livid, wretched body of the dead Christ, lying on the bare earth, and around it, petrified in their grief, with mute gestures, grimaces, tears that would never end or bring solace, the friends and relatives who had gathered: the Madonna, St. John, Joseph of Arimathea, Simon, the Magdalene, two holy women. And as I looked I remembered Aunt Malvina, who, at this sight, could never restrain her tears. She put her black, old maid's shawl to her eyes, knelt, not daring (as she would have liked, poor thing!) to make her unbaptized nephew kneel as well.

Finally, I recovered myself and turned to leave.

And there, kneeling gravely in the distance, in a pew of the central nave, I glimpsed Carlo Cattolica, the only worshiper in the whole church.

My first impulse was not to disturb him, to go off unseen. Instead, with pounding heart, I tiptoed along the left nave until I was level with him.

His pack of books at his side, he was praying, his pure, handsome brow resting on his joined hands, offering, to me who observed him, the same finely chiseled, inscrutable profile he turned to me every day in school. Why weren't we friends? I asked myself, in torment. Why *couldn't* we become friends? Was it perhaps because he didn't respect me enough? No, it couldn't be that: Boldini and Grassi, though good and intelligent, were surely no more so than I. Was it because of my religion, then? But the difference of religion had never arisen between me and Otello. On the contrary, at the Fortis', though they were all very devout, militant members of Catholic organizations (Signor Forti belonged to the St. Vincent de Paul Society, and Giuseppe had also joined it two years ago), no one, ever, had reminded me that I was a Jew. What's more, Cattolica's parents, as far as I knew, unlike the parents of Otello and Camurri, weren't known for being particularly devout. Why, then? Why?

Cattolica stood up, crossed himself, saw me.

He came toward me.

"Well! What are you doing here?" he asked me in a whisper.

"I was looking at the *Pianzún d'la Rosa*," I answered, pointing my thumb in the direction of the carved group.

"Ah, didn't you know it?"

I knew it, I explained, because I had seen it often as a child in the Chiesa della Rosa; and I went on, as we returned together to look at the statues, about Aunt Malvina and her passion for visiting churches, all the churches of the city.

This information seemed to interest him. He wanted to know who this aunt of mine was. Was she by chance my mother's sister?

"No, my grandmother's," I answered. "My maternal grandmother's, she's a Marchi."

In the meanwhile we had come outside in the open

space in front of the church. It was now almost nine, and that space and Via Borgoleoni, especially in front of the door of the Guarini, were filled with young people. Side by side, we leaned against the red façade of the Gesù. And since none of our classmates seemed to have noticed us, we went on talking. It was the first time. The event excited me, stimulated my talkativeness, my need for intimacy.

What did we talk about? Religions, naturally. He asked me if it was true that we "Israelites" didn't believe in the Madonna, if it was true that, in our belief, Jesus Christ wasn't the son of God, if it was true that we were still waiting for the Messiah, if it was true that "in church" we kept our hats on, and so forth. And I answered him, point by point, with feverish, exaggerated enthusiasm, not even noticing how elementary his questions were, how generic and vulgar, not to say insolent, his curiosity was.

At the end, I asked him a question.

"Tell me," I said, "have you . . . I mean your family . . . always been Catholics?"

"I should say so," he answered, with a brief, proud smile. "Why?"

"Oh, I don't know. Cattolica is the name of a town, a town on the coast near Riccione . . . between Riccione and Pesaro . . . and Italian Jews, as you know, all have the names of towns and cities."

He stiffened.

"In the first place, that's not correct," he replied at once, showing that, on this point, he was perfectly informed. *"Many* Israelites have the names of towns and cities, but not *all.* Quite a few are called Levi, Cohen,

Zamorani, Passigli, Limentani, Finzi, Contini, Finzi-Contini, Vitali, Algranati, and so on. So you see? I could also cite countless cases of people with last names that *seem* Jewish, but aren't Jewish at all."

Saying this, he started off, pursuing the subject in a low voice. This allowed us, for once, to enter the door of the Guarini and then go down the long corridor to our classroom and, finally, to cross the room to our desk, walking side by side, together, like close, affectionate friends.

IV

I remember very well the arrival of Luciano Pulga, the first Monday after classes resumed.

Everyone was seated in his place, waiting for Professor Guzzo to arrive and dictate to us the Greek text to be translated (Monday began with two hours of Guzzo, invariably devoted to written work; but he, the "great man," liked to linger at times by the big window at the end of the corridor almost till nine fifteen, immersed in apparent contemplation of the overgrown lot at the foot of the Gesù's apse), when, in the door, instead of the professor's gigantic form, we saw appear the tiny figure of a blond boy in a green sweater, gray shorts, long tan stockings. Who was he? A new acquisition, obviously, even if he had no books under his arm. Anyway, as he stood hesitantly just inside the door, seeking an empty place with his bluish gaze, the intense, cold blue of an Alpine glacier, I somehow felt, at once, repelled by his physique, like a little wading bird's, with his thin legs, his beaklike nose, and yet I was moved, at the same time, by his anxiety to find a nest. I looked at him. Seeing no one beside Giorgio Selmi (Chieregatti was absent that day), he first tried to sit at the second desk of the first row. He was rejected: that place was not free, Selmi informed him at once—it belonged to somebody who was absent, but who tomorrow or the next day, on returning to school, would surely throw him out. At this, without insisting, he stood up and moved off at once. Thin, with a scrawny Adam's apple which trembled, half choked, just above the collar of his white shirt, he began looking around again, ending finally at the back of the girls' row, at the very desk, now vacant, where in the beginning I had wished to exile myself. He went down the aisle between the second and third rows, walking fast, determined, staring straight ahead, like somebody who finally sees a port. He was perspiring, however: little drops of sweat beaded his skin above the sinuous, slightly receding edge of his upper lip. And this detail, the little drops of sweat (I noticed it in a flash, as he went by, almost grazing me), again gave me a vague feeling of revulsion.

I also remember well what happened after Professor Guzzo's entrance into the room, with the professor subjecting the newcomer to a long interrogation ("My God! Who are you?" he began. "An auditor, perhaps?"), and the boy answering, "Pulga, Luciano," responding to the tyrant, displaying a fluent, convincing manner of speaking, very Bolognese, like a traveling salesman's. The class, cowardly, underlined Guzzo's remarks with loud, collective laughter; and finally I rose to the poor boy's aid, since he was guilty of having come to school with only a fountain pen; I not only offered him the regulation paper necessary for him to be allowed to do his written work, but also accepted willingly Guzzo's invitation to move to the last desk, so that "Signor Pulga, Luciano" could use my dictionary.

And I remember finally the curious sensation that

remained with me all through that first hour and a half spent side by side with him, with Pulga, working to solve the puzzle of the Greek translation. Professor Guzzo, on making me change my place ("Since you've gone so far as to offer him some paper," he said, "go a bit further, and retrace your steps to your point of departure . . ."), Professor Guzzo insisted that the dictionary was to stay always on the top of the desk, in full view and squarely in the middle, so that neither of us would be able to copy. But Pulga copied, all the same, whenever and whatever he chose. Exploiting the professor's slightest moments of distraction, he cast rapid, devouring, sidelong glances over the Schenkl, displaying a technique, I thought, whose perfection suggested years and years of practice, a long career. Well, the fact that he should copy from me with such complete faith, with such absolute dismissal of any thought of personal judgment, intent only on carrying out his plagiarist's job without technical errors: this, I repeat, filled me with a complex, entangling sentiment, a mixture of pleasure and repugnance, against which, even then, I found I had no defense. I was virtually unable to react.

When we went out at noon, I found him at my side.

Could I take him to some bookshop? he asked me. At the Minghetti Lyceo, in Bologna, where he came from, they had used mostly different textbooks, and so, unfortunately (as if his father hadn't had to spend enough already for the move!), he now faced the painful necessity of buying almost all new ones. A disaster! If he could at least buy them a few at a time, or on credit . . .

We walked up Via Borgoleoni together, in the pale January sun, and Pulga, respectfully putting me on his right, went on talking. Though Guzzo, in class, had drawn from him almost everything about his family and his scholastic background, he now repeated, for my benefit, that they came from Lizzano in Belvedere, a big mountain town above Porretta Terme, some sixty miles from Bologna, where his father had been the village doctor for about ten years; and he, personally, had completed his elementary schooling in Lizzano, the first years of Ginnasio in Porretta and the last in Bologna, going back and forth on the train every blessed day; and finally that his family, made up of four people—father, mother, and two sons—because of this transfer to the province of Ferrara, which had come out of the blue, were having serious problems at the moment. Just imagine: they still hadn't found a house!

"What!" I exclaimed, appalled. "You don't even have a place to live?"

It seemed impossible to me. The idea that a doctor's family, one on the same social level as mine, should be without a roof seemed to me not only incredible but frightful.

"Where are you staying, then?"

"At the Hotel Tripoli, in the big square behind the Castle."

Oh, I knew quite well what sort of place the Tripoli was! It wasn't so much a hotel as a third-class restaurant, frequented at noon by peasants and cattle dealers, and, in the evening, by what my mother would call "bad women." The bedrooms were upstairs, on the second and third floors. And the owner (a little fat man with a bowler pushed back on his head, a toothpick between his gold teeth, who, in the summer, always sat in his shirt sleeves by the front door, astride a kitchen chair) rented them out, mostly by the hour, digging the keys from his pocket.

"Of course, it's not one of the best hotels," Pulga went on to say. "In fact"—he snickered—"at night it's a bit active. But still it costs money, you know, real money! You want to know how much we spend, by the day, for four people, board included?"

"I've no idea."

"Fifty lire."

"Is that a lot?" I asked, unsure.

"A lot? Just figure it out: five times three, fifteen. It comes to a total of fifteen hundred lire a month. That's plenty, isn't it? When you think that at Coronella my father, as village doctor, gets a basic salary of a thousand a month . . ."

I was distraught.

"How do you manage, then?"

"Well . . . I said a thousand lire as a base salary. Then there are house calls, operations, especially operations. But you know how it is, people in the country, before they'll dig into their pockets and pay . . . They'd rather die! And there's the competition of the Central Hospital here in Ferrara. Coronella is too close to the city. Six miles is nothing."

Suddenly he stared at me with his steady, ice-blue eyes.

"What's your father's profession, if I may ask?"

"He's a doctor, too," I said, embarrassed. "But he doesn't practice."

"Doesn't practice?"

"No. He makes an occasional house call, but he

doesn't charge . . . he only sees friends. Sometimes they send for him from out of town, too. For circumcisions," I added, with some effort.

He didn't understand, and turned to look at me. But he recovered himself promptly.

"Ah, yes, of course . . . So your family has a private income, I imagine."

"I suppose so."

At the Malfatti Bookshop, on Corso Roma, the textbooks he wanted were all sold out. They would have to be ordered, the clerk explained, and this late in the season they probably wouldn't arrive for at least two weeks.

I expected this news to upset him. Instead, he was relieved, or so it seemed to me. With his handkerchief he wiped the drops of sweat that the shop's heat had brought out again between his nose and mouth, and he gave the clerk the list of volumes. He would come back in two weeks, he said, and with that he preceded me toward the exit.

He insisted on walking me home. By now it was almost one. I tried to discourage him, pointing out that Via Scandiana was far off, and that if he saw me home he wouldn't get back to the hotel before two.

"Oh, don't worry!" he cried, laughing. "That's the one good thing about eating in a restaurant: you can turn up when you please."

"Don't you eat with your family?"

"Yes, of course . . . in theory. But Papa comes in from the country only in the evening, after his office hours; and Mamma is always out hunting for an apartment. . . . So we're really only together at suppertime. It seems strange to you, doesn't it?"

He looked at me and laughed, shifting to one side his slightly protruding jaw (a sure sign of *"mauvais caractère,"* my father always said). And it was obvious that he envied me, yes, he envied the order, the economic security, the middle-class stability of my family, but at the same time he also felt some contempt for me. For the same reasons.

He was surely afraid of having revealed himself. Suddenly, in fact, he began to thank me very effusively for the help I had given him during written work in class. If I hadn't been there to lend him a hand, he said, God knows how he would have managed; and with characters like Guzzo, it's the first impression you make that's important, enormously important. By the way, why didn't I ask him, ask Guzzo, for permission to move permanently beside him, at the last desk, or, if not permanently, at least until he had got all his books? That Cattolica, my desk-mate, looked like a very nice boy, very polite; no doubt he was bright, terribly bright. And yet, to tell the truth, he didn't find him likable. Didn't Cattolica give himself airs, perhaps? His manner, his way of looking at others, had a certain . . .

He broke off.

"I hope I haven't offended you," he said, peering at me. "Maybe you and he are great friends. . . . Are you great friends?" he asked, anxiously.

I avoided looking at him, and answered: "No, not especially."

As far as his books were concerned, I went on, he needn't worry. At school I could always lend them to him. But, when it came to moving to his desk, I wasn't sure I could do as he asked. It wasn't that Cattolica and

I were particularly close. Still, we had been together for more than two months, and to drop him now . . . how could I? After all, we got on well together.

"But whom do you do your homework with? With him?"

"No, I don't study with anybody."

We were almost home. We came from Via Madama into Piazza Santa Maria in Vado, and turned down Via Scandiana. What was that sort of embankment down there at the end? Pulga asked me, as we went on walking. And with his raised arm he pointed to the mist-blurred prow of the Montagnone, against which Via Scandiana seemed to come to an end.

I stopped at the door of the house, pressed the bell, and turned to explain to him what the Montagnone was. But now Pulga's attention was attracted by something else.

"My God!" he exclaimed, seriously. "It's a whole building!"

He stepped back to the center of the street, to take in the whole façade.

"Is it all yours?"

"Yes."

"It must have lots of rooms."

"Yes, quite a few . . . Counting the upper floors, about fifty."

"And your family lives in them all?"

"Oh, no. We live on the third floor. There are tenants on the floor below."

"So you and your family live in about twenty rooms, is that right?"

"Well, yes . . . more or less."

"How many of you are there?"

"Five. Papa, Mamma, and three children: me, my brother Ernesto, and my sister Fanny. And you have to count the maids."

"How many do you have?"

"Two . . . plus one who comes in by the day."

"Twenty rooms! I can imagine what it must cost to heat them. And the tenants?"

At that moment the lock of the front door clicked. I looked up. My mother was at the window.

"Why are you so late?" she asked, looking at Pulga. "Come up. Papa is already at table."

"Good afternoon, Signora," Pulga said, with a slight bow.

"Good afternoon."

"This is a classmate of mine," I said. "Luciano Pulga."

"I am so happy to meet you." My mother smiled, then said to me: "Come up now, or Papa will be angry."

She drew back and closed the window. But Pulga still couldn't make up his mind to leave. He went to the door, pushed it slowly, and stuck his head in the opening.

"Can I come inside for just a moment?" he asked then, turning. "I'd like to take a look at the garden."

He preceded me, in silence, across the threshold, dutifully removing his little cap. Then, without taking his eyes from the end of the vestibule, which opened on to the garden, he tiptoed two or three steps forward. I watched him. He walked on the broad, waxed pavement of green and white tiles, with that slightly wooden caution of a little, solitary swamp bird.

He stopped. He continued looking straight ahead, in silence, his back to me.

My lips moved mechanically. I said: "Do you want to come back and do your homework with me, this afternoon?"

V

My mother was happy I had found a new friend.

She liked Luciano very much, right from that first afternoon. When she came into the study he not only rose to his feet, but also kissed her hand. This gesture, performed with remarkable skill, won her at once. A little later, in fact, she returned with the tea tray—an exceptional tea, complete with butter, honey, currant jam, toast, slices of fruitcake—and sat down to watch us eat; meanwhile, as she conversed with Luciano, her brown eyes caressed him with a maternal expression. She asked him about himself, about his family, taking an interest in his father's professional problems, sharing his mother's anxiety in searching through the city from morning till night for an apartment, and offering, on this score, all her own help. Poor signora! she sighed, if she needed anything she was to telephone, absolutely, for Mamma would be happy to help, and to put her women friends in action.

"What a sweet boy that classmate of yours is," she said that same evening, at table. "*He* is polite, well brought up!"

"*He.*" She was obviously contrasting him to Otello Forti, whom she had jealously found always too "rustic" and "glum." Irritated, I didn't answer. It was true, I thought, staring at my plate, that instead of studying at home I had always preferred to go to the Fortis', on Via Montebello. But what of it? How could he, Otello, be blamed, if, ever since Signor Roncati, at the elementary school on Via Bellaria, had placed us side by side at the first desk in the central row, just in front of himself, I had always enjoyed studying at Otello's house? When it came to hand kissing, social airs, and graces, Otello was worthless, true enough. But he was frank, sincere: perhaps even too much so. . . .

Signora Pulga did telephone, and my mother promptly reported what she and the signora had said to each other.

In a very faint voice, weary but very likable, the signora had thanked her profusely. First she said that she had already found an apartment (outside Porta Reno, on the Bologna road, or, in other words, also the road to Coronella) so, as far as that went, these kind people needn't worry about them any more. But her Luciano! How could they, she and her husband, ever forget what all of us were doing for her Luciano?

"Thank you, dear signora, thank you with all my heart," she had concluded. "At present we still have to arrange our furniture; you can't imagine what it costs to keep it in storage. But in two weeks or so, my husband or I will take the liberty of disturbing you again with a phone call. My Osvaldo, as a doctor, would like so much to meet your husband!"

"As a doctor!" my father grumbled, with a grimace, but still visibly happy, as he was whenever anybody remembered his medical degree. "Just wait and see, he'll be wanting a loan. . . ."

Doctor Pulga didn't want a loan at all, at least not from my father. A few days later, when he came (without wife) to our house, he spoke out clearly: he had come, he said, only to meet a "colleague" and to have a little chat. Then he began talking about himself. He had studied medicine in Modena, between 1908 and 1913; in 1914 he had married; between 1915 and 1917 he had fought on the Carso, and in 1918 at Montello; in 1920, because of lack of funds, he had had to become village doctor at Lizzano in Belvedere, which, after almost ten very hard years, he had decided to leave, to take on the same post at Coronella, near Ferrara. He felt the medical world in Ferrara, unlike Bologna, wasn't controlled by a tight little clique, keeping it closed, hermetically closed, against any "infiltration." He knew all of them, you might say, the Bolognese doctors: old Murri, Schiassi, Nigrisoli, Putti, Neri, and Gasbarrini. The surgeon, Bartolo Nigrisoli, was in fact a friend of his family.

Short, with a red "cyanotic" face, with green, bulging "Basedow" eyes gleaming behind his little pince-nez, Doctor Pulga, my father declared, hadn't appealed to him at all. What a gossip, he said, claiming to be a friend of this one and that one, in Bologna, on intimate terms with half the university and half the Sant'Orsola Hospital, and then how his tongue wagged, sparing no one! Bartolo Nigrisoli, for example, today perhaps the best man with a scalpel in all Italy, had always been an anti-Fascist. So there was nothing wrong if he stuck to his ideas. But to wish, instead, as Doctor Pulga had had the impudence

45

to wish, that he might be dismissed from the Bologna "classes," where his teaching risked "corrupting" so many young men (and declaring himself Nigrisoli's friend, all the same, and friend of his family): it was monstrous, it really was! And finally, was it conceivable to come calling and to stay, sunk in an armchair, from half past three until eight? He was to be avoided, for heaven's sake! If by chance Doctor Pulga telephoned again, he must be told one of two things: either that the master was out, or else that he was in bed, in bed and asleep!

But Luciano? What was Luciano like?

Physically, to be sure, that first impression of slight repugnance had remained; seeing him daily had not erased it. Though he looked very clean, his clothes perfectly neat, there was always something about him that disturbed me; perhaps it was the little drops of sweat that appeared at the slightest emotion, in the blond down of his upper lip, or else the blackheads scattered all over the waxy skin of his face, but thicker at the temples and at the base of the nostrils, or else the sharp, sideways movement of his jaw when he pronounced the letter "z," or else, I can't say, the yellow calluses that strangely hardened his large, thin hands, somewhat like a hunchback's. But otherwise I must confess that, especially at the beginning, his refugee humility, his total submission as an inferior and a protégé, gave me an almost intoxicating satisfaction. My relations with Otello had never been easy, really. He tolerated my superiority but made me pay for it in many ways: with his constant glumness, his mulish obstinacy, with coming to my house, the few times he deigned to, always reluctant, sighing, huffing.

And here, instead, was a completely different sort, for whom my house (he told me, that first day, when I took him from room to room, to visit the apartment) was the most beautiful, comfortable, and welcoming he had ever seen in the world, my mother the nicest and kindest of mothers, and I, when it came to homework, a kind of monster of brilliance and intelligence, an oracle to be listened to in religious silence. Though he wasn't stupid or inept, and during the question periods of that first month, when he was interrogated by all the professors, by Guzzo and by la Krauss, by Bianchi, and by Razzetti, the history and philosophy teacher, he had defended himself tooth and nail—in fact, even Mazzanti, though against his will, hadn't been able to give him a mark lower than five —he allowed me to unravel the difficulties at my ease, dictate aloud what I chose, merely, at the end, while he was still writing in his notebook with that broad, neat, somewhat angular and feminine handwriting, bursting out in cries of approval, of respectful admiration, such as "Bravo!" "What an ace!" "I've never seen anybody translate Greek like you!" "You're lucky!" and so on. How calm it was, how restful, I said to myself, with Luciano Pulga. What a difference between him, who never opened his mouth (in fact, I did the translation alone, so that if my mother tiptoed up to listen behind the door— and it was possible that she did: more than once I had heard the parquet in the next room creak—she would have heard only one voice, mine), and Otello, who, when he opened his mouth, did so only to contradict or to play devil's advocate! But leaving Otello out of it, if I had succeeded, as I once wished, in becoming part of Cattolica's group, just imagine how difficult life would have

47

been for me! The rivalry that separated us at school, fanned by the inevitable presence of the two cronies Boldini and Grassi, would certainly have continued at his house. At Cattolica's house, to be sure, since on this point, on the place where we would study, there could have been no argument allowed. Either his place, or solitude: take it or leave it. . . .

Luciano arrived, every afternoon, around four, and he never left before seven thirty or eight. Still, we didn't study continuously, of course. Apart from the half-hour devoted to tea, we broke off also to talk from time to time. And here it was Luciano who decided when; it was he, suddenly energetic and authoritative, who decreed moments of pause for my poor fatigued brain, and then, later, when he felt it had rested and been sufficiently diverted, he directed me to start work again.

During the intervals, in any case, he made every effort to entertain me, distract me, even make me laugh. He owed me a great deal: for the protection I had offered him since the first day, the books I was still lending him, the hospitality of my home, the assignments which, practically speaking, I did for him. And he, he seemed to say, paid me back with the modest but not despicable gift of his presence, of his encouraging witness. Was this little? Perhaps. However, I must be sure of one thing: he could give no more.

He was careful to boast of nothing. Very often he declared he was without ambition, happy, for his part, to remain within the "limbo of those who hover between a five and a six," because—he smiled—attracting attention, whether for good or for bad, meant you had to "pay" in the end; it was as if he said: "I know I am worth little, indeed, less than little." And yet, in the way he talked to me about the school, casting doubt, for example, on Mazzanti's fairness toward me (according to him, between me and Cattolica, Mazzanti "sided" shamelessly with the latter); or else hinting to me that from down there, at the last desk—an inconvenient place, no doubt, but still with some advantages—he had a much clearer, more objective view of the class than I could have, involved as I was in the competition, in the struggle, in the glorious but also petty daily effort to shine: in every sentence of his, I felt, understood, his firm conviction that he was useful, perhaps indispensable to me.

Rightly convinced it pleased me, he missed no opportunity to speak ill of Cattolica.

In his opinion, Cattolica was simply overrated, full of hot air. Present company excepted, could I compare the intelligence of, say Boldini, or even Giorgio Selmi, to Cattolica's? The fact is that Boldini set no store by being first (acting as henchman is also a vocation), and to Selmi it meant even less, since he aspired to nothing higher than a seven average, which meant exemption from tuition fees. A grind, like Chieregatti, only better organized and more clever: that's what Cattolica was, after all, and the proof lay in the fact that Guzzo, who was nobody's fool, didn't allow himself to be dazzled, like la Krauss and Razzetti, by mnemonic displays; when he wanted a slightly unusual answer, he generally skipped Cattolica, because he knew *whom* to ask. True, I had no gift for scientific subjects, or rather, to be more precise, I was able to apply myself only in subjects I liked: Italian, Latin, Greek, et cetera. But all I would have to do was try a little (hadn't I passed the repeat mathematics examination with an eight, last year?), and he was willing to bet that even in mathematics, physics, and natural science, "Signor Cattolica" would bite the dust.

"No, no, I don't think so," I parried, weakly. "I've never grasped mathematics."

"You've never grasped it because you've never *wanted* to grasp it."

"Maybe. But doesn't it amount to the same thing in the end?"

"It is *not* the same thing. Ability is one thing; will power is another."

"If you ask me, it's a question of cerebral matter, of a kind of brain that's not suited . . ."

When I dropped these words, smiling, Luciano protested vigorously. How could I utter such absurdities? he cried—I, of all people!

From the way he looked at me, serious, extremely respectful, I realized he was only awaiting my permission to remind me of the mathematical virtues of my race (my father also, who was very good at figures, was convinced that we Jews were the best mathematicians in the world, blaming, fairly seriously, my lack of talent on the peasant blood of my grandmother Maria). In any event, I pretended not to understand, and let the subject drop.

But he was right: little by little he was proving indispensable to me. And I remember, on this score, an afternoon toward the end of February when Luciano, because of the snow, was late in coming.

No longer expected, the snow began to fall that morning, just after nine, and from inside the classroom it was beautiful and exciting to see the little flakes glide silently in slow descent against the blackish background of the Gesù, and then, on coming out, to find Via Borgoleoni all cloaked in white. There was the usual turmoil, a general snowball battle, during which, for once, Luciano and I lost sight of each other; but it made no difference, it was understood that around four we would meet as usual.

After lunch, instead of letting up, the snow became thicker. At five, oddly uneasy, I was already wondering if Luciano would manage that day to come on foot from the distant Foro Boario neighborhood to Via Scandiana. Perhaps not, perhaps he wouldn't make it, I told myself, looking out of the window; perhaps I had better start studying by myself.

I sat down at the desk, but the light that fell from the green lampshade on the notebook and the open volumes (the dictionary and the text of the first book of the *Iliad* at my left by my elbow, and the notebook closer, almost against my chest, in the same position as the sheet of paper on which I am now writing), the soothing, bluish light of the lamp did not help me concentrate. The Pulgas, at their house, I reflected, didn't yet have a telephone. Still, if he really planned not to come, Luciano could presumably have found a way of letting me know, going to telephone from the grocery, fifty yards from his house. When there was some urgent need, that was the phone the Pulgas used; he had told me so himself.

I opened the window and stuck my head out, sniffing the air and looking down. The snow went on falling, but sparser now, a kind of fine, dancing dust, without weight, around the yellowish light of the street lamps. Down in the street an even, compact blanket, immaculate, had covered and leveled everything. There were no cobbles, no sidewalks: nothing could be distinguished.

And there below, as my heart, mad with wild beating (mad with a joy mixed, as usual, with irritation), leaped to my throat, I suddenly recognized Luciano, yes, Luciano, at that very moment, slipping rapidly through the downstairs doorway.

VI

In the early days, when he wanted to distract me, Luciano counted on two equally inexhaustible repertories: either he told me jokes in Bolognese dialect or else he delved into the memories of his childhood. These, like the jokes, were prevalently comical. Entirely concerned with Lizzano in Belvedere, and with the mountain localities around Lizzano (Porretta, Vidiciatico, Madonna dell'Acero, Corno alle Scale: names that soon became familiar to me), they always presented him as the true protagonist, even when the apparent protagonists were his father, his mother, or Nando, his brother. The role he assigned himself was always the same: the sly one, the wise, the clever one, quick not only with his wits but also with his hands or his feet. Perhaps the stories were only inventions, fantasies, but what of it? I was amused, I laughed as if I were watching the farces of Ridolini or Charlie Chaplin. And Luciano was pleased, too, with his performance and with its success.

Later, however, the subjects of his talk changed.

It began by chance. One March evening, I think it was, an evening when a violent storm had broken out.

At seven I saw him stand up.

"Are you leaving already?" I asked him.

"I think I'd better."

"Do you want to stay for supper? If you like, I'll go tell Mamma."

He stared at me. He had begun to tie up his books with their strap; he paused.

"Thank you . . . thank you so much," he stammered, shifting his jaw more than ever. "But I wouldn't want to be in the way."

"What are you talking about? I'll go tell them."

I got up and ran to the door.

"Wait a moment!"

I turned. Standing by the table lamp, he seemed paler than usual: with his dark blue eyes, hollowed deeply by the shadow, in his small, bony face, and, in the light, the top of his beaklike nose and his protruding forehead.

"No, don't. They're expecting me at home."

I insisted that it would be easy to telephone the grocer near his house.

"All right, then, but after supper . . ." he said, hesitantly, still staring at me. "I can't stay here overnight."

I hesitated. I didn't like the idea of sharing my room with him.

"Why not?" I said, with an effort, coming back toward the table. "We could put a cot in my room."

He didn't answer. He went over to the window and peered through the panes.

"Is it still raining?" I asked.

"I think it's tapering off."

He came back toward the center of the room and sat down in an armchair.

"It was really much better when we lived at the Hotel

Tripoli," he said. "It was more convenient, and more amusing, too. Living out by the Foro Boario will be nice in the summer, I suppose; but in winter it's worse than Lizzano. It's the new walls, probably; the house is cold, and you can't imagine how damp!"

I asked if they didn't have central heating.

It was a banal, indifferent question. And yet, as I asked it, something, I didn't know what, suddenly warned me of an imminent danger. All at once I felt we were sliding toward an intimacy that, until then, we had kept at a sufficient distance: an intimacy I *had* to refuse at all costs.

But it was too late now. Luciano was already explaining to me how his father, instead of radiators, whose installation for the moment was beyond their means, had thought of buying two terra-cotta stoves. This kind of stove worked very well, provided, however, that the pipes rose vertically. But his father, like the "stubborn idiot" he had always been, had decided to run the pipes from one room to the next, horizontally along the walls. Result: if you lighted so much as a scrap of paper the house immediately filled with smoke. It was enough to asphyxiate you.

I started: at that "stubborn idiot," and at this sudden abandonment, on his part, of all reserve and caution. What had happened? I asked myself, frightened. What was happening?

Though I remembered the disastrous impression Doctor Pulga had made on my father, I tried to defend him. But Luciano went right on. Not only was his father an idiot, he repeated, he was also miserly and violent. I should let him have his say, after all. Often, when his father came home in a bad mood—and this happened frequently—he gave the whole family a beating.

Were these also inventions, fantasies? Perhaps. How, in any case, could they be made to fit with his earlier stories, which depicted a heroic Doctor Pulga, climbing, at night perhaps, accompanied by his little son, to a remote Apennine farmhouse, to learn, on arrival, from the astute peasant that it wasn't his young wife who was in labor, but his cow, also at her first birth? Still, it wasn't the truth that mattered, not even now. What mattered was the changed tone with which he addressed me, the sudden harshness, without any tact, the rude bitterness in his voice.

"What!" I said, breathless. "Does he beat even . . . your mother?"

Oh, he beat her especially, that swine, Luciano exclaimed—though, he added with a snicker, perhaps she was the one who was looking for his blows. His mother, after all, liked being beaten: that was the *real* truth. And he, his father, had realized that perfectly, he satisfied her, as best he could.

Luciano burst out laughing.

"Mysteries of the human heart!" he exclaimed. "You think only men are revolting? Women, too. Oh, yes, indeed! Women, too!"

The Hotel Tripoli, he added, was better also for this reason (apart from the radiators' operating at full blast): because it offered a very exact picture, without "gilding the lily," of life, of real life. Had I ever seen the owner, that pig with a German name, Müller, always down on the ground floor, sitting behind the cash register in the restaurant, with a toothpick between his metal teeth?

Couples who wanted to "take a little afternoon nap," for example, didn't even have to come and eat. They had only to go straight over to him, among the tables, and he would promptly hand over a key. What a laugh it was to see them, the couples, as they showed up! Ordinarily they were country men, following "cheap whores," who had picked them up in the square; but sometimes there were youths from the city, who came in first, taking the key and vanishing up the stairs, to be followed, a minute later, by her, the "chicken," who slipped inside "looking guilty as sin." Chicken? Hardly! Instead of some young thing, often it was an "old hen" of forty: already a mother, perhaps even a grandmother, and sweating guilt from every pore of her leathery face. They were the wives of engineers, lawyers, doctors: you could recognize them with your naked eye. Ladies of the highest society, who, most likely, that same evening would turn up at the Teatro Comunale or, the next day, march in uniform along Via Cavour, boldly wiggling their behinds *"coram populo."* It really was a riot.

The alarm clock, on the table, said seven thirty. The parquet in the next room creaked. My mother looked in at the door and observed us contentedly.

"Have you finished?" she asked.

I looked at her in a daze. Yes, I confirmed, we had finished.

Luciano had sprung to his feet with his usual promptness.

"Poor thing!" my mother said, commiserating. "To have to go on foot, in this rain, beyond the Docks! Do you have an umbrella? And galoshes? If you'd like to stay for supper, you know you're welcome."

"Thank you, Signora," Luciano answered. "But as I was saying to him"—and he nodded toward me—"I'd rather not. Papa and Mamma, if I don't turn up at home . . . well, they're upset. You understand."

My mother insisted. It would be easy to telephone, to ask Papa and Mamma's permission, wouldn't it? Still Luciano didn't allow himself to be persuaded. They spoke: he standing by the armchair, more prim and affected than ever; and she, from the doorway, enfolding him in the caress of her brown gaze. Still sitting, I looked first at one, then the other. I followed the movements of their lips, but most of their words I didn't understand, I didn't hear.

Finally my mother withdrew.

"I promise you it was a lot of fun, very entertaining," Luciano began again, in a whisper, as soon as he had made sure, with a glance, that the door was shut tight; "but mostly it made you laugh."

And at night, he went on, the Hotel Tripoli teemed like a railroad station! He slept with his brother, Nando, who no sooner hit the bed than he was off, and not even cannon-fire could have waked him, so he heard nothing, "the baby," neither their parents' fights every evening in the next room, before they went to bed (fights that often ended in blows), nor the various sounds that filtered through the thin wall opposite. In that room beyond, "work" went on constantly. During the whole night there were moans, sighs, creaks: a disaster, if you were trying to get some sleep. But who could think about sleeping? Only that dope Nando, in fact; Luciano didn't give it a thought. He stayed awake until very late, in his nightshirt, his ear glued to the wall, spry as a cricket, alert at catching, through the change of voices, the various "changes of the guard." On some nights, in the next room, as many as five couples followed one another in rapid succession. Every so often he got up and went to see.

"To see!"

"Of course. Through the keyhole of the communicating door."

"But what . . . what did you see?"

"What did I see? Oh . . . I didn't always manage, worse luck, because the bed in there was right in front of the keyhole, and what's more, it was high, very high, you know how those big double beds are. But don't worry: I still managed to see something!"

Once, for example, he went on, he had seen a back rise above the bedstead. It was a woman's, and it went up and down, "um-pa, um-pa," as if she were seated on the back of a trotting horse. Another time the couple walked around the room, naked, so each time they passed the keyhole, they showed him their "front" and their "behind." Another time a couple, instead of on the bed, preferred to make love on the rug, just near the door. And that time, though he desperately twisted, trying to look down, he saw nothing, but to make up for it he *heard* more distinctly than he ever had before: which, perhaps, all things considered, had been even better.

"What do you mean, better?" I stammered.

"Oh, a thousand times better! Besides the moans and the stifled cries, you should have heard what they said to each other. My God! They couldn't stop."

At that moment the maid came into the study. She announced that supper was on the table, so Luciano was forced to break off and leave.

But the following days, stealing more and more time from our studies, he went back to that kind of talk. I was weak, passive, unable to react; and he, realizing this, took advantage.

He told me, among other things, that he was reading a wonderful book, which he had secretly taken from his father, *Aphrodite*, by Pierre Louÿs—a wonderful book, he explained, for two reasons: for its literary beauty and for the "highly educational" contents. He told me how he was forced to read only a few pages at a time, at night mostly, in bed: one hand ready to turn the page, and the other, below, equally ready to accompany the salient points of the narrative with a "quick shake of the old rod."

"Will you lend it to me?" I asked.

"What?" he asked, snickering. "The book?"

I nodded.

"Well . . . if it's the book," he went on, looking at me with his blue enamel eyes, "I don't know if I can. My father is very fussy about his books. He sets great store by them!"

To be able to "put his paws" on that and on other equally interesting books his father kept on a shelf in his study, he continued, he had to wait until night as a rule, when everybody in the house was asleep, being careful, afterward, to put everything back in its place. With this "trick" he had managed to read almost all the novels of Pitigrilli, *The Garden of Tortures* by a French author whose name he had forgotten, *Sex and Character* by Weininger, and *I promessi sposi*, not Manzoni's, obviously, which had already been a sufficient pain in the ass during the last two years of Ginnasio, but the other book, written by one of "my faith," Guido Da Verona, who, in his opinion, was much better. In any case, he added, raising one hand as if to block any protest from me, in any case Louÿs's *Aphrodite* beat them all hollow, all the books he had mentioned. The first part of the novel—did I want to know what it described? It described a garden, the garden around the temple of the Goddess, where dozens and dozens of women "did it, full-throttle, with men and also among themselves." And they invented so many positions and ways that even he, who, all modesty aside, understood these things pretty well, was dumfounded.

I had never masturbated then. When he learned this, Luciano was profoundly surprised. What, he exclaimed, at my age! He, on the contrary, since the age of ten, had always masturbated regularly: at least once a day.

"But doesn't it harm you?" I asked.

"Harm you! No, it's very good for you. Maybe," he smiled, "if you do it too much, it saps your memory a little. But can you imagine how it opens your mind?"

According to him, to develop one's mental faculties, there was nothing more "suited." You shouldn't go to excesses, of course, just as you shouldn't overdo with wine or, say, sports. Still, it was good to do it. It was a normal, natural thing, and nature, if you knew how to interpret "scientifically" the impulses it arouses in us, cannot want our harm. But, on the other hand, was I sure that circumcision hadn't diminished my "sexual sensitivity"? Had I ever had erections? And at night, when I was asleep, had I ever waked up "wet"?

I answered as best I could, also admitting when I didn't understand very well: namely, that, yes, often, at the most unlikely moments, my "thing" stiffened, and once or twice I had waked up in the morning with my pajama bottoms damp.

One afternoon Luciano unbuttoned his shorts and showed me his member. Then he wanted me to do the same. Ever since my childhood I had been terribly modest, and I was reluctant. But he insisted, and I finally complied.

He looked at it carefully, leaning forward a little, with a detached air, like a doctor. What, practically speaking, did circumcision amount to? he asked. Until then he had believed it was an operation of a certain importance, consisting in the removal of an actual piece of "flesh." On the contrary, as he now realized, it was a very simple matter. After all, what difference was there, between his and mine?

And, for the purpose of verifying what, in fact, this difference was, he unbuttoned himself again.

We came to Easter, with the constant sensation, on my part, of being thrust gradually toward something unknown and threatening, though nothing specific ever happened. Luciano talked and talked, never stopped talking. His voice held me fast, it gripped me in its low, buzzing coils.

I have few precise memories of that period. I lived as if in a tunnel, without glimpsing its end; if anything, I feared I would suddenly find myself facing it. I remember my feeling of base complicity at each appearance of my mother in the room. And I remember also one afternoon, during the Easter vacation: not a real afternoon, perhaps, perhaps it was only dreamed.

I went to play football at the parade ground, behind

the Aqueduct, with about half the class. We began around two o'clock, happy to run breathlessly on the dry grass seared by the winter frosts, happy to be free of our heavy clothes, happy in the fine sunshine that brightened even the grim sheds of the army warehouses and glistened on the mossy marble of the statue of Pope Clement, usually so melancholy in its solitude, and gilded the bluish distances of the first houses of Via Ripagrande and Via Piangipane. Around three, Luciano also arrived, on foot, naturally. Like Cattolica, he cared little about playing; and besides he was too frail, too thin, no captain would want him on his team. Stamping his feet to keep warm, he stayed at the edge of the field, acting as public. While we played, his comments reached us every now and then: he would applaud, or boo, or jeer. Every time I looked at him, even from the distance, I thought I saw him smile, I could sense more than see the smirk on his little, dead face. And I knew why he was staying. Because of me. After the end of the game, he would want to climb on the handlebars of my bike and direct me to Via Garibaldi, to the corner of Via Garibaldi and Via Colomba, and from there we could conveniently observe the people going in and out of the nail-studded doors of the Pensione Franca and the Pensione Mafarka.

By then it was growing dark. And suddenly, when we were about to quit, I fell and hurt my knee. It was nothing serious, I knew that quite well, but I let a moment go by before standing up—"faking," in other words. I lay there, supine, my eyes closed, my aching limbs slowly pervaded by an extraordinary sensation of well-being; I was glad the game ended because of me, glad about my accident, and glad that three or four companions, gathered around me, were making feeble efforts to get me to my feet. I listened to their calm voices, high in the cold evening air above my outstretched body, and I wanted never to rise again.

"Oh, he's not dead," somebody said at last. "Can't you see he's faking? Come on, let's go get dressed."

I heard their footsteps move away, and I opened my eyes a crack. I peeped through my half-lowered lids. Erect, in silence, beside me (enormous, seen from below, gigantic; coldly, looking me up and down, as if I were an object), only Luciano remained.

VII

The day before school reopened, I came down with tonsillitis.

I've always been subject to it, from my earliest childhood (for this reason Aunt Malvina took me so often to visit the Church of St. Blaise, the patron of those with sensitive throats). That year, however, the inflammation seemed much more serious than usual. Perhaps it was an abscess, my father diagnosed, and my Uncle Giacomo, immediately summoned by my mother, was of the same opinion.

To operate? Not operate?

Agreeing about diagnosis, my father and Uncle Giacomo regularly quarreled about treatment. And so, to settle the eternal argument of the family's two doctors at my bedside (Papa was for operating, my uncle opposed), Mamma thought it best to send for Doctor Fadigati, the city's best specialist: the same doctor who had operated on my tonsils when I was a child, though, to satisfy my uncle, he had removed only a part of them.

Fadigati came promptly, examined my throat, confirmed the diagnosis. When it came to risking "a little operation," he, too, like my uncle, felt that for the moment, with "the fever," it shouldn't be considered. Watch and wait: this was the only course to follow at present. After the seventh or eighth day, the abscess would be ripe, and then they could decide: whether to delay further, allowing the "sac" to drain by itself, or whether (at this point the doctor reached out and patted my cheek, smiling at me, kindly and reassuring), or whether to seize the occasion and finally take out "the whole lot."

There was no need. The abscess burst on its own, sooner than foreseen. As for the removal, then, of the two stumps of my tonsils, it was decided once again that nothing should be done. They would go into the matter at the end of the school year, before we left for the sea.

Freed from the imminent threat of the scalpel, I breathed easier. And yet I was not content; was irked, in fact, by the faster cure, which hastened my return to school. I thought with apprehension of Luciano. Contrary to my expectation, during the whole period of my illness he had come to visit me only once. It was the second or third day, when I was still running a high fever. He had sat down primly at the side of my bed, conversed in a a low voice chiefly with Mamma, but even when she left us alone (actually, she came and went constantly) he had talked only about school questions: what point they had reached in the translation of the *Iliad,* which of Horace's *Odes* Guzzo had assigned, what la Krauss was explaining at the moment, and similar things. I was silent, listening. At a certain moment, expressing myself with some effort, I asked him if by any chance, in view of my illness, he hadn't felt it advisable to go study with someone else, at least temporarily. To which he answered no, with an affectionate smile, it hadn't even occurred to him "to be unfaithful to me." Who did I think he was? A Judas? I was to worry about getting well, though. As soon as I was cured (I wasn't to be upset, meanwhile, about our studies; smart as I was, I'd catch up with the others in no time), then the two of us would immediately resume our "winning combination." And it was this very prospect, especially, that filled me with obscure reluctance during the next few days. School, and Luciano: resuming the former meant, perforce, resuming with the latter.

Resuming with Luciano: what did this mean, really?

From my bed, convalescent, I abandoned myself, without restraint, to strange thoughts. I retraced slowly the dark tunnel of the past months: from the morning when Luciano appeared for the first time on the threshold of the classroom, to when, from one subject to the next, we had taken up the "hand-job" matter, as he would call it. I knew quite well how it had been able to happen. Everything stemmed from that question of mine about the central heating; the rest, including the mutual display of members, had come as a rapid consequence, on its own. I could see the scene again. After having persuaded me to reveal myself, Luciano had bent over to look: with an impassive expression, yes, but also—why not admit it?—a little disappointed, as if I, so much more stocky and sturdy and athletic than he, should necessarily be bigger there as well. And I, I asked myself now—I? Surely, I, when he had unbuttoned (I would never have supposed that such an insignificant character could hide in his pants a *thing*—a thing, indeed: there was no expression more suited to defining it!—so out of all proportion: swollen, white, but, especially, huge), I, for my part, had felt my stomach seized by an irresistible disgust. After that, I had done nothing but think of it, really: of that sex, obscenely, frighteningly enormous, and of my disgust. Disgust, revulsion. If I were to begin again with Luciano, I would have to face the disgust of every minute spent with him. Far more than just Latin and Greek!

And if I were to break with him? What if I invented some excuse and shook him off my back?

At home, I could perhaps get away with it. I would have only to tell some story, blaming the cause of the break on Luciano perhaps, or inventing a quarrel. Mamma, almost certainly content simply with the fact that I would go on studying at home, wouldn't bother about anything else. But at school it would be different: at school it wouldn't be so easy. Even though, in front of the others, I had always been slightly ashamed of my friendship with Luciano (up in la Krauss's laboratory we sat side by side, unfortunately, but when Mazzanti, before grading him, felt called on to consult me, most of the time I didn't answer and just shrugged my shoulders, annoyed), still everyone in the class knew he came each afternoon to do his homework at my house. And then there was Cattolica. There was Giorgio Selmi. Cattolica had always pretended not to notice, he had let me pair off with that "ass-licker Pulga" (so Luciano was called, in general, by the old A section cliques) without ever giving me the satisfaction of mentioning it to me, so if I were to break now with Luciano, Cattolica's triumph would be too great, too complete, too hard to swallow. As for Giorgio Selmi, recently, in gymnastics class (Luciano was excused because of the aftereffects of a child-hood pleurisy), he had had the hypocrisy to come and complain to me of his own solitude and offer himself as my desk-mate for the coming year, so Giorgio Selmi also had to be held at bay. To break with Luciano now, at once, would have meant giving way to Giorgio too quickly, an ignoble submission.

I returned to school, and Luciano immediately started coming to the house again.

I had been ill, I had to make up the lost time, so it was easy for me, those first days, to keep him at bay ("Let's cut out the chatter!" I ordered, with authority). Still, I knew we would soon lapse into the old subjects, oh, I knew that well. This was guaranteed by the vaguely sardonic expression I saw in the depth of Luciano's eyes and, even more, by certain imperceptible changes in his behavior: he flattered me much less, for example, and he allowed himself moments of distraction which, before, would have been inconceivable, and also, when I worked doggedly at a sentence perhaps not as troublesome as I made it out to be, he would hum softly, as he waited. "Go ahead, if it really means all that much to you," he seemed to say. "But does it mean that much, really? I can guess, never fear, what interests you *too*, by now."

But then one afternoon something new happened.

I had gone to our gymnastics period in the gymna-sium, which was separate from the school, on Via Praí-solo, having agreed first with Luciano that we would meet at my house around six. At five, on coming out of the gymnasium, I can't remember which of our class-mates produced a rubber ball, and immediately, in the vast yard in front of the building, we improvised a foot-ball game. More than a real game, it was a series of confused scrimmages, with no rhyme or reason. But so it went. The firm order that I was not to become over-heated, the same order that a little earlier, during gym-nastics, had kept me sitting on a bench, now filled me again with painful, searing envy. My back against the high wall that separated the yard from Via Praísolo, I went on watching the others run, jumping, shouting, sweating, and more than ever I felt an outcast, a weak-ling, a wretch. Completely worthy of making a pair with somebody like Luciano Pulga.

And yet I was not alone.

Cattolica, too, instead of going straight home as usual, had stayed to watch. Leaning against the wall like me, he had lighted a cigarette and wasn't saying a word. Suddenly, however, he came over to me, and—an extraordinary thing—he slipped his arm beneath mine.

"You're sorry you can't play, aren't you?" he said, sympathetically.

I answered truthfully: I had a tremendous longing to play, but unfortunately I couldn't. I had been ill re-cently and—I added, superfluously—my father, who was a doctor, didn't want me to sweat, under any cir-cumstances.

Cattolica listened to me with great attention and patience. Much taller than I, he bent his head forward slightly to hear me: a pose habitual with him when some-thing or somebody aroused his interest.

"Excuse me if I'm prying," he said finally. "But

70

what was wrong with you? I didn't follow Pulga's daily communiqués," he added, ironically, "but I think he mentioned a sore throat."

Daily communiqués? I thought. But Luciano visited me only once, and, oddly enough, he had never even telephoned to ask after me!

"I had an abscess," I answered.

He frowned, with an expression of suffering.

"Is that painful?"

"Fairly," I said, smiling and looking at him. "I wouldn't wish one on my worst enemy."

He blinked.

"I'm sorry," he said. "If I'd known, I'd have come to see you, too."

Despite that "too," and although I was on guard, my heart leaped up. Cattolica, at my house! The touching picture of him, the repentant rival, distressed, at my sickbed, rapidly came into my mind. But I still didn't believe him, I didn't trust him.

"It hurts terribly," I said, pretending to be completely absorbed in the painful memory of my sort throat, "especially the first few days. It looked as if they would have to operate, but then, luckily, the abscess burst on its own. Anyway, they'll probably have to operate on my tonsils. Not now, of course, but in June, before we go to the seaside."

We went on conversing in this vein, side by side, for a few more minutes. Though Cattolica in the meanwhile had freed his arm from mine, I still felt his presence beside me, looming, urgent. What did he want? I asked myself, my face toward the courtyard. And I was doubly anxious: because of what he might want and, at the same time, because of my self-imposed obligation to behave well, with dignity.

"I know you live around here," he said at a certain point.

"That's right," I said, "on Via Scandiana. Not far from the Palazzo Schifanoia. Have you ever seen the Schifanoia frescoes?"

"No. Two or three Sundays ago I went to Mass, at Santa Maria in Vado, near there, but that's all. We live over by the station, on Via Cittadella."

"You do?" I asked, hypocritically.

"It's a very pleasant neighborhood," Cattolica went on, with the unshakable confidence he displayed whenever he spoke of his possessions: *his* dictionaries, *his* fountain pen, *his* Majno, and—who knows?—perhaps even *his* fiancée. "New . . . modern." He broke off. "Say," he added, "why don't you come and do your homework at my house, today?"

I raised my eyes and looked at him, amazed.

"At your house!"

"Why not?" He smiled, pleased at having dazzled me. "You can go home, pick up your books, and then come to me: Via Cittadella 16. It won't take long, with your bike. Ten minutes at most."

"Thanks, thanks a lot," I answered, "but tell me, don't you study with Boldini and Grassi?"

"Well, yes," he confessed, like a gambler who, admitting defeat, shows his cards. "But what does that matter?"

"Oh, nothing, naturally . . . Just that there are three of you already; a fourth might be one too many."

From the way he stiffened his back and looked away, I realized he had misunderstood me. He thought that I was blackmailing him, setting a condition: them or me.

He answered that I was quite wrong: one more would make no difference at all, since he had a huge table in his room at which—and he smiled proudly—the whole class could have studied, if necessary, the girls included. But then, joking aside, he added, besides the fact that Boldini and Grassi, as he could assure me, would have no objection to me, to my presence, the three of them had been studying together now for too many years for him to . . .

He looked into my eyes.

"You must understand," he concluded.

I understood only too well. Between Boldini and Grassi, on the one hand, and me, on the other, he naturally could choose only them, his old friends, his faithful vassals and followers. Moreover, it was equally obvious, a foregone conclusion, that between his house and mine, it was *his* house, *his* room, *his* table which I, no less than he, *had* to prefer. My house, with all it might contain, was an unspecified place in the city, which he, from Via Cittadella, hadn't the slightest notion of taking into consideration as something definite, really extant, as a roof beneath which I and my family actually lived. And what about that "ass-licker Pulga," who came there every day, to my house? He, too, did not exist; Luciano also was an abstract, negligible entity: a painful, embarrassing subject on which it was not worth spending even a word.

"I understand, and I thank you," I answered. "But, really, today I can't. Pulga's coming to my place, so how could I? . . . If I were able to telephone him . . ."

"Doesn't he have a phone?"

"No. Not yet. He lives far away, near the Foro Boario, beyond the Docks, and it's hard to reach him by telephone. I'd have to call a grocer, near his house. But it's better not to. If I call too often, the man might become angry. And besides, it's late. Pulga doesn't have a bike; he's probably already on his way."

Without saying anything else, we started, in tacit agreement, toward the exit. At the gate we stopped, hesitant. I had to turn left; he, right.

"Good-by then," he said coldly, holding out his hand.

"Aren't you going to wait for Boldini and Grassi?"

"No. They both have bikes. I'm taking the trolley."

"Unless . . ." I went on, still holding his hand, ". . . unless I could bring him, too. I could go home first, tell him, and then we'd come."

It would have been a solution, I thought, looking into his face with ill-concealed eagerness. After all, it would have been a magnificent solution: for me, too.

"What do you say?"

"Him? Who?" Cattolica asked, with a contemptuous grimace, withdrawing his hand. "Pulga?"

"Yes, of course. Didn't you say your table was so big? If four of us could work there, then . . ."

He reacted clumsily.

"No, for heaven's sake! Five of us! And Pulga! Are you joking?"

"Joking? Why?" I answered, very calmly. "What is there about Pulga, after all, to make the three of you treat him as if he had the plague?"

I felt mortally offended, and I wanted to know.

74

"He's been coming to my house every day since January," I went on, "and, as far as I know, he hasn't given me bubonic plague!"

But he was right, I couldn't help thinking, even as I went on—Luciano really did have the plague, and I, too, from being with him, had caught it.

Cattolica pursed his lips.

"*De gustibus*," he said. "You're free to have anyone you like at your house. As I said, if you want to come to my place, fine, but as for him—never. I should think not!"

"Well, if that's how it is," I murmured in a trembling voice, on the brink of tears, "too bad. I'm sorry. But it's both of us, or nothing."

VIII

That evening Cattolica and I parted brusquely, or rather it was he who dropped, between us, a curt "good-by," turning his back and hurrying off toward Corso Giovecca. Still, the next morning in class, and then in the following days, he persisted, without referring to the strange conversation we had had, but for that very reason giving me the impression that the question had by no means been shelved. On the contrary, he buzzed around it, I realized, waiting to resume the subject at the first opportunity. Meanwhile he worked hard at removing the invisible barrier of rivalry, of prejudice, and of pride that had separated us until then.

When speaking to me, during classes, he was careful not to turn his head. He continued to show me his firm, medallionlike profile, his eyes fixed, as always, on those of the professor seated on the dais; but he would cover his mouth with his opened hand and whisper behind his fingers. He was too disciplined and eager, he set too much store by his reputation also for good conduct, to neglect these elementary precautions. And yet the perfect rigidity of his neck and trunk, which I also tried to imitate, I realized, was directed not so much toward the eyes of the man in front of him (even if it was "that dragon Guzzo!") as to those, far more dangerous because beyond his surveillance, of the students behind him. If Luciano, from his desk back there by the wall—so I reflected, with a shudder—were to notice that between Cattolica and me there was no longer the same coldness as before, or at least that now we talked, did nothing but talk, he might also be able to guess, sly as he was, the *true* subject of our whispers. It was fairly absurd, on my side; but the fact was that I felt so guilty toward him, I could almost feel physically on the back of my neck the chill of his blue, inquiring gaze.

It is easy, therefore, to imagine my bewilderment when, one morning, Guzzo himself called on Cattolica by surprise.

He was reading aloud a poem of Catullus, the one that begins: *Multas per gentes et multa per aequora vectus* . . .

Suddenly he stopped, and ordered, in a grim voice: "Continue, Cattolica."

Cattolica started, then put his hand to his chest, as if to ask: "Me?"

"Yes, you, sir," Guzzo confirmed, becoming even more formal in his wrath. "Continue the reading, if you please. We want to see how you manage."

Cattolica began to leaf desperately through the book, which was, indeed, open, but not to the right page. And his torture would have gone on for God knows how long (immobile at the other end of the desk, I didn't dare help him) if at a certain point, from behind, Malagù hadn't raised his hand, to help.

"Good for you, Malagù," Guzzo remarked. "I see you are following the lesson, that our good Catullus interests *even* you. . . . But, Cattolica, tell me: doesn't Catullus interest you? You dislike him?"

"No. . . . It's not . . ." Cattolica stammered, very pale, as he rose slowly to his feet.

"No?" Guzzo said, with feigned wonder, arching his great brows which were drawn at the base of his broad Wagnerian brow like two gray circumflex accents. (He was an atheist, a "pagan," as he had proclaimed many times; and he missed no opportunity to tease anyone, like Camurri and also Cattolica, whom he suspected of belonging to a clerical family.) *"Passer deliciae meae puellae,"* he declaimed sweetly, winking simultaneously at the rest of the class: "is it that little amorous jest you reproach him for? You can't forgive him?"

"I like it very much," Cattolica said, in hot denial. "Only I . . ."

"Only you," Guzzo interrupted him, "for some time now, exploiting—not without hypocrisy—my trust, have taken to coasting. *Costicamus*, yes, *costicamus*. Your attention has been very marginal indeed. I see you, you know, you and your neighbor, talking constantly, *sub tegmine manuum*. You especially! What's wrong with the two of you? Do you feel (erroneously) that you have both passed the course already? Or is it spring you feel?"

Cattolica turned, as if to invoke my testimony. But he said nothing. He looked back toward Guzzo, whose eyes, meanwhile, were carrying out a slow survey of the desks.

"I wonder," Guzzo said finally, "if it wouldn't be wisest to proceed at once to the separation of a couple, like you, which is all too congenial by now. In any case, my dear Cattolica, you have been warned. If I catch

78

you chatting again, I shall send you back to the last desk, beside our saintly Pulga, Luciano. You understand?"

And, having taken out his fountain pen and opened his ledger, he plunged into writing a long note of disapproval.

In the street, we didn't even attempt to be alone, since, once outside, the usual groups formed, and Luciano, also, was prompt to cling to my side, often not leaving me until he had accompanied me halfway down Corso Giovecca, to the corner of Via Terranuova. But apart from the afternoons when we saw each other at gymnastics (there were at least two more), we began telephoning each other, usually in the evening, before going to bed.

What did we talk about generally? I don't know; I've forgotten.

I can assume we talked about our teachers, our classmates, the books we were reading (we had quite different tastes: I preferred adventure stories, cloak-and-dagger tales, Dumas, Ponson du Terrail, Verne, as well as *The Children's Encyclopedia;* he was more serious and read popular science works and fictionalized biographies): we discussed things of no real importance, in other words, considering what was in the offing. But could it have been otherwise? The sound of our words was the ink with which the cuttlefish clouds the water around himself, to escape a snare. Sheltered by that vocal ink, like two cuttlefish, we went on studying each other, grazing each other, extending cautious tentacles.

But what Cattolica told me about Boldini and Grassi, on the other hand, I remember exceptionally well.

Contrary to all my expectations, Cattolica showed a

strange independence of judgment toward them. Boldini, he thought, unquestionably had "a fine brain"; but he lacked imagination, the brilliance that always accompanies real intelligence. He was very neat, punctual as a Swiss clock, excessively precise. He was too closed in on himself, his character was too egoistic. In the six years that the two of them had known each other, Cattolica had never managed to have a real conversation with him, a logical discussion; every attempt on his part was always answered by the usual grunts, the usual whistling between the teeth, the usual sudden slaps on the shoulder. He was strong, true, very strong. It wasn't a lie, for example, that last month, with the thermometer practically at zero, he had swum across the Po at the Giarina beach. But, all things considered, he was a mediocre person; and his cult of physical vigor (Didn't I know? Every morning Boldini worked out for half an hour with dumbbells!) was the most compelling proof of it. As for Grassi, though, in thought and character, he was the opposite of "that other one," he wasn't worth much either. He read a lot, he knew all sorts of things, but finally, when you came right down to it, what did he get out of it? A great mental confusion. That's what! Boldini never read a book except those assigned for school; and he was wrong, of course. But Grassi was even worse; he read too many, and at random, so that his head was crammed with odds and ends, and his eyesight grew steadily worse. Good? With that sickly, Silvio Pellico air of his, he wanted very much to seem good. He was sincere, basically, a friend you could rely on. . . . Maturity, balance, harmony of the various faculties of spirit and body, ability to aim steadily at a goal: these were qualities both lacked, Boldini and Grassi equally.

Through these criticisms of his, it was evident he meant to put me and himself on a different, superior plane, ready, in order to achieve his end (but was this really the end he was pursuing?), to praise indirectly that brilliance and imagination that characterized my intelligence, perhaps, but surely not his. I did not rise to the bait, however. Hearing him express himself in that way about his best friends, the very ones with whom, then, during written work in class, he went on collaborating as closely as before, I distrusted him more than ever.

I repaid him by speaking well of Luciano. He was by no means a fool, I said, or even the hypocrite everyone thought. I understood how he might seem rather unpleasant, to look at, and even I, at the beginning, for that very reason, had had to overcome considerable inner resistance. But if one were to choose one's friends only on the basis of physical appearance, mankind would be in a bad way! I exclaimed. So much for Christian charity! When Pulga arrived in Ferrara, I went on, moved, in spite of myself, he was all alone, like a stray dog. He didn't know anybody and he lacked everything: even the books to study with. His family, then, didn't have a house; they lived, or rather camped, at the Hotel Tripoli, on Piazza Castello. Under those circumstances, could I refuse him the help and hospitality he needed so badly? To be sure, even though you took him for his true worth, and though he wasn't a fool (that was just his manner: he assumed a dull attitude more out of laziness than anything else), the profit one could derive from studying with him was not great, I admitted that. Still, intellectual faculties, too, did not represent the true bond of friendship.

"And what, in your opinion, does represent the true bond of friendship?" Cattolica asked me at this point, one evening.

We were talking on the telephone. His words, preceded by a little sarcastic laugh, took me by surprise.

"I don't know," I answered. "It's hard to say. How is it that two people become friends? Because they fundamentally appeal to each other, I imagine. But—may I ask?—why are you asking me this question?"

"Just because," he said, mysteriously. "No real reason. I only wanted to hear your enlightened opinion on the subject. So then, the true bond of friendship consists," and he snickered again, "in a reciprocal liking. Am I right?"

"Of course," I insisted.

For the moment he said nothing else: neither in favor of the idea, nor against it. But the following evening, again on the telephone, he brought the subject up once more. He began by declaring that he had given a lot of thought to what I had said the day before (I, too, that afternoon, being with Luciano and feeling, once again, repugnance and fear rising within me, I, too, had been unable to avoid thinking about it). Well, yes, it was correct, he went on, assuming that "head of the class" tone which often made him so odious to me, friendship and love as words in Latin have the same root: *am*; and if love, *amor*, is, practically speaking, desire to harmonize, to identify oneself with the loved one, to feel with the other (*sun-pathèin*), it's obvious that this fellow feeling, or *simpatia,* is also the basis of friendship. But would I allow him to ask me another question?

"Go ahead."

I sensed, over the wire, a slight hesitation on his part. Then he said, "Let's be frank," in a curiously breathless voice. "Do you really like Pulga?"

"Why, yes," I answered, with relief, laughing, "I've told you that already. Why shouldn't I like him? He isn't an ace; at times he is even a little boring and obnoxious; but basically he's a good sort. You, you and all the others, promptly slammed the door in his face only because . . . Who knows why? And, instead, poor thing, he really didn't deserve such treatment."

I was sure he would agree with me, admitting at last that he was wrong and apologizing. But instead he didn't accept my accusations in the least.

"Have you ever been to his house?" he asked.

"No, why? He always comes here. . . ."

"And . . . tell me . . . ," he went on, hesitant again. "While we're on the subject of reciprocal liking . . . do you think that he likes you?"

I was struck by the question and, even more, by the tone of his voice: uncertain and furtive, first, and then, all at once, determined; like someone who, long torn between two paths, one smooth and easy, the other difficult of access and dangerous, finally decides on the latter. I didn't understand. What was he getting at?

I answered that I had every reason to believe (I tried to laugh again, at this point, and I succeeded) that my liking for Luciano was returned.

"Are you really sure?" he said, gravely, insinuatingly.

"Yes, I am. As I said, he was always the one to seek me out. If he didn't like me, instead of coming every single day to my house, he'd go to somebody else, wouldn't he? For instance . . ." I added, ironically, "to your house."

He sighed. "You're so naïve!"

"Naïve?" I asked. "Why?"

But he didn't want to explain his reason for considering me naïve. So, to persuade him to speak, or rather— using the same phrase he used—to spill once and for all everything that was bothering him (I should hear Pulga, *my* beloved Pulga, he blurted out finally, and the fine things he was saying about me, behind my back!), I had to insist for quite a while.

IX

"Really, you are *too* naïve," Cattolica said. "And that's the very reason why his behavior makes me so indignant. I hate being forced into this role, believe me. But if you could hear him, *your* beloved Pulga, and the fine things he goes around saying about you, behind your back!"

I realized at once that he wasn't bluffing, that what he said was simple truth. And though the news, in its cruelty, wounded me deeply (my heart almost stopped beating), still I nearly burst out with a joyful "at last," yes, a cry of joy. Here was the opportunity to free myself of Luciano, I thought in a flash. Here it was, at last!

But I restrained myself. "I don't believe it," I said sharply.

"I was expecting that," he said. "But if you want proof, I can give it to you."

I didn't answer him, I hung up. I was convinced he would call me back. Closed in the telephone closet, in the dark, I waited for a few minutes. In vain. Suddenly the door opened, and my mother's face appeared in the luminous aperture.

"What are you doing, sitting there in the dark?" she asked, examining me with a worried look.

"I was telephoning."

"Whom? Cattolica?"

"Yes."

"How is it the two of you have called each other so often, these past few days?"

Instead of answering her, I grazed her cheek with a kiss and wished her good night.

It was very hot in my room. As soon as I had come in and locked the door after me, I went straight to the window and flung it open. It was a beautiful starry night, with no moon, but very bright nevertheless. Down in the garden the trees were outlined distinctly: the magnolia closest, the fir farther on, and, at the opposite corner, where the arches of the vestibule ended, the linden. Among the flower beds, the milky white of the gravel; and in the center of the path, also whiter, which opened before the dark cavity of the vestibule, a black, motionless dot: a stone, perhaps, or maybe Filomena, the centenarian family tortoise who, as Mamma had gaily announced at supper, had emerged from hibernation. "Hey, Filomena," I called absurdly, in a stifled voice, "hey!" But the black dot, stone or tortoise, didn't move.

I drew back, I undressed slowly, and, without closing the window, I lay supine on the bed, my hands clasped beneath my nape. I was naked, inert. From the garden rose an intense perfume, of trees, grass. I was thinking of Luciano, naturally, and I was more sure than ever that Cattolica hadn't lied. Of course! I said to myself, filled with the wrong Luciano had done me, and at the same time continuing to feel light, happy, freed of a great burden. Of course! I repeated. How could I have been so blind, not to realize by myself that Luciano was a traitor? I tried to become indignant, outraged. "The pig!" I muttered, my teeth clenched. "The beast!" Tomorrow, at school, I planned, I would face the Judas at once. I would ask him brutally: "So that's how it is, is it? So it's true that you say bad things about me?" and, without waiting for him to deny or confirm it, I would slap him in front of everyone. I could visualize the scene: myself, flushed, eyes bulging, fists raised to strike, in James Cagney style; and him, the little wretch, the ignoble, cheap gangster, caught in the act, writhing at my feet, trying to protect his bruised, swollen face with the backs of his hands; and the others, in silence, making a circle around us. I was fierce, killing him with my blows. Luciano didn't defend himself; he simply protected his face with his hands, showing me their repugnant callused palms, and he didn't cry, either; he just took his beating.

In my imagination I saw myself striking him mercilessly; and in the meanwhile my member had stiffened, as when, a child, through the half-opened door of the kitchen I watched, unseen, the cook (her name was Ines, a huge, placid country woman, with a maternal manner) while she disemboweled a chicken.

The next morning, as soon as I woke from a dreamless, leaden sleep, everything took on a different dimension. I was still determined to exploit this opportunity to break with Luciano, freeing myself once and for all from the slavery of the monstrous nightmare that for such a long time had clouded, secret and unconfessable, my days; but my role of executioner seemed immediately absurd to me, very difficult to carry out. And with Luciano, in fact, who was standing waiting for me at the corner of

Corso Giovecca and Via Borgoleoni (he was waiting for me, without any doubt: the minute I saw him I was seized by an obscure feeling of guilt and of fear), I was careful to behave as usual, as if nothing had happened. We started walking together toward the Guarini, in the blue morning, cool and sunny, talking of this and that. From time to time I peered at him. He was smaller, weaker than ever, even more wretched in his gray flannel shorts, with his skinny, flamingo legs. But his high, protruding forehead, the seat of so much treachery (Cattolica had mentioned proof: well, yes, only with tangible proof in hand would I manage, perhaps, to attack him!), I could hardly bring myself to look at that brow.

Along the entrance corridor, in the usual morning crush, I glimpsed Cattolica. He was walking with Boldini and Grassi, tall and slender between the two of them, and he gave me a serious, reserved look. I pretended not to have seen him. In the classroom, however, as we were waiting for the lesson to begin, it was he who spoke first.

"A fine way to act," he said, with offense and disgust in his face. "May I ask why you hung up on me, last night?"

"I'm sorry," I murmured. "I don't know why myself."

"Do you or don't you believe what I said to you about Pulga?"

Pale, thin, he stared at me with his black eyes, glowing fanatically in their sockets: the eyes, I thought, of a medieval monk. I realized he was driven only by a desire to humiliate me; but I needed him, now, and I could make no other choice.

"I'll believe you," I answered, "when you've given me the proof."

The professor, I don't remember who it was, came in, and we had to be silent. But in the course of the morning, shielding, *more solito*, his lips with his hand, Cattolica returned to the subject several times. It was hard to talk like that, in spurts, being careful, as we were, not to be caught, but we did talk all the same. I was right, he began, quite right to demand proof. If that was all I wanted, in any case, I had only to come to his house.

"To your house!"

"Certainly. I'll have Pulga come too, and then you'll hear some fine things!"

"What is it he says, after all?"

"If you expect me to tell you," he answered, with a grimace of disgust, "I'm afraid you'll have a long wait. I detest gossip. Ugh!"

"Hear?" The idea of a confrontation, now, frightened me. "How?"

"Just come. I have a very precise plan to make him talk. Never fear."

"When . . . when should I come?"

"This afternoon, if you like."

"At what time?"

"Oh, anytime you want," he said considerately, "whenever's convenient for you. At four, five, six, seven . . . As I said, come when you like. You only have to"—he smiled—"tell me the time exactly. You understand why, don't you?"

I pointed to the backs of Boldini and Grassi.

"Yes," he confirmed. "They'll be there, too. They have to be."

I still hesitated, but in the end I agreed. I said I would get rid of Pulga on some pretext, and at six, without fail, I would be at his house.

"Be punctual," he insisted. "Otherwise, you might meet him at the door."

At the exit, Luciano came up to me. I was calm now, determined.

"Listen," I said to him when we reached the top of Via Borgoleoni, "you'd better not come today."

He raised his eyebrows. "No? Why not?"

In the entrance hall of the school, a little earlier, I had seen Cattolica say something to him; he had answered, then nodded, in silence. The hypocrite! I thought now. How good he was at pretending, the repulsive worm!

"I have an appointment," I answered curtly, avoiding his blue gaze which was seeking mine, a bit anxiously. I stared at the drops of sweat that were beading his lip.

"An appointment!"

Yes, I nodded. Then I went on, in one breath: "I have to go with Mamma to my Uncle Giacomo, to be examined."

"What for?" he asked. "Has your sore throat come back?"

"That's it," I said, pretending to swallow with difficulty. "I think my uncle wants to give me some injections. Papa is against them, but my uncle insists. He hardly ever prescribes anything else."

He stared at me with a strange expression: saddened, grim. As if he could guess I was lying. As if he had guessed everything.

"I see," he said. "What time are you going to your uncle's? If, by any chance, you're going there late, then I could come a little earlier than usual: about three, or three thirty."

"No. Better not. I don't know exactly when my uncle can see us. When he has office hours, he's very strict: you just have to wait until he telephones he's free, and this can happen at any time in the afternoon, early or late."

We had stopped to talk at the corner of the Corso, at the same place where I had met him that morning; and there we separated, I turning left as usual, and he, this once, not accompanying me to the corner of Via Terranuova but going on, instead, toward the square and Porta Reno.

At six precisely, I rang the bell at Cattolica's house.

He came to the door himself (he didn't even greet me), and it was he, when we had gone down the three cement steps in front of the door, who took my bicycle on his back and led me into a little entrance hall.

Outside, it was still light; I had crossed the city from east to west, with the low sun in my eyes. But in the little entrance hall of the Cattolicas' house, without windows and dimly lighted by a single bulb of a few watts, it was dark, you could hardly see. It was a cold, bare vestibule, which smelled of damp: the floor was of dark tiles, shiny and slippery; there was an enormous, old-fashioned coatrack against the wall beside the street door, then a bare, skeletal stairway, of cement like the three steps outside, rising in an angular spiral to the floor above. And opposite, under the stairs, a glass door, ajar, beyond which you could glimpse a pantry crossed by a melancholy shaft of sunlight. Piled one on top of the other, against the coatrack, were three bicycles. One, the first, was Cattolica's, the gray Majno. He added mine to the pile, then, changing his mind, he put it on his shoulder again.

"What are you doing?" I asked in a whisper.

"It's better to take it into the pantry," he said, also whispering, and heading for the glass door. "Sly as he is, he would surely notice it."

"Are the others here already?" I asked again, recognizing the bicycles.

He had already vanished into the pantry.

"What?" he asked, raising his voice.

"I was asking if Boldini and Grassi are already here."

He reappeared.

"Of course," he answered, and didn't look at me, carefully wiping his hands with his handkerchief.

With him in front and me behind, not exchanging another word, we climbed the steps until we reached, at the top, a kind of antechamber, even more narrow and bare than the vestibule below, and as if suspended above it. From the single window, which apparently overlooked Via Cittadella, an uncertain light penetrated the pink curtains, as faint as the artificial light on the floor below. Set against the rear wall, opposite and parallel to the iron railing which, like a balcony's, marked the stairwell, I glimpsed, here too, a black coatrack, laden with dark garments. At my left, two doors, both shut; but through the cracks in the wood, and through the keyhole of the nearer door, there came a blood-red, violent, vivid light.

Having opened the door, Cattolica, his back to me, plunged into that light.

"Come. Come in," I heard him say.

X

Though dazzled (it wasn't electric light, as I had first supposed, but the sun, which, close to setting, struck the room obliquely), I went in, looking around in a daze.

The room was large: a kind of drawing room, in fact, with a broad horizontal window at the end, which took up half of the wall, with a western exposure, and a second, smaller window, facing south, toward Viale Cavour, the Aqueduct, and the meadows of the parade ground. But immediately, the moment I was inside, I noticed, besides the presence of Boldini and Grassi, seated against the light at a large rectangular table, books and notes in front of them, two bookcases of blond wood, one facing the other, filled with handsome bound volumes, and a shiny black leather sofa, in the center, with a low table and two armchairs of the same leather opposite, the impeccably waxed parquet, almost totally hidden by rugs, and beside the door, the bed with a soft woolen blanket carefully folded at the foot, and a charming little table at the head. In short, I saw the luxurious appearance of the room, surely by far the largest and most beautiful of the whole house, compared to which even my study, so admired and praised by Luciano, looked like a closet. After all, he hadn't exaggerated, Cattolica, I thought, when he had boasted of his table, insisting that the whole class, girls included, could have sat around it. And once again, sensing behind that luxury, like a little nabob's, the determination of parents prepared for any sacrifice so that he, their adored son, might achieve the most radiant goals in his career and his life (especially the determination of his mother, a mathematics teacher; I had seen him come to school on her arm some mornings: a tall woman, pale, thin, with darting eyes, hollow cheeks; she was capable, so we heard, of giving as many as ten or twelve private lessons in a day), once again I was gripped by the obscure dislike tinged with envy that from the beginning I had felt toward my desk-mate.

After having exchanged a simple "hello" with Boldini and Grassi, I sat down at one end of the long, narrow table. I had, opposite me, Boldini's head, half hidden by a large lamp with a green silk shade, Grassi on my left, and Cattolica, who had also sat down and had begun speaking rapidly, on my right. I was uneasy, filled not only with anxiety about Luciano's arrival, which I believed imminent, but also with distrust and bitterness. Cattolica, however, seemed neither uneasy nor anxious to inform me of his plan. He chatted volubly, entertaining his guest, the outsider. He would gladly have offered me something, he said, his black eyes sparkling feverishly, but (and, after all, it was better so) we were alone in the house, his mother wouldn't be back before nine. . . . Now he summed up, he justified himself. He said he was sorry, really sorry. It had never been his habit, his "style," to use "devious ways": even with characters on the level of "a" Pulga. On the other hand, it wasn't entirely his fault. In the past few days, as I would have to admit, he had done his best to make me open my eyes by myself. And how had I repaid his efforts? Not only had I turned, to the end, a deaf ear, but I had also assumed a certain attitude toward him, as if, instead of Pulga, he himself were the real traitor and swine. And so, finally, he had had enough. Realizing that anything he said would be misinterpreted, and unable to bear any longer the position of someone trying slyly to come between two friends, he had decided that the only way to convince me of his good faith was to have me touch reality, like St. Thomas. Now I understood, thank God, and I believed him. Still, I should ask him—he pointed to Boldini—or him—he pointed to Grassi. Was it true or wasn't it? he asked the two of them, not giving me time to draw breath—was it or wasn't it true that Pulga, the three or four times he had come to study with them (it had happened a month ago, roughly, during the ten days or so of my illness), had constantly said the most odious things about me? He seemed capable of nothing else except sitting there, where I was now seated, copying their work for all he was worth and slandering me at every opportunity. And I should bear this in mind: he railed against me spontaneously, of course, without *ever* being encouraged, showing such pleasure in saying all sorts of things about me that he, Cattolica, once had been unable to refrain from asking him if, by chance, I had behaved badly, had done him some wrong. To which the miserable creature had been so bold as to say no, oh no, that I, as far as that went, had never done anything to him; but this fact still couldn't prevent him from judging me "objectively" (*objectively*, had I heard that?) for what I was and for what I was worth.

I listened without answering. When Cattolica, feverishly pointing his bony index finger, had urged me to
turn to Boldini and Grassi, I had obeyed him passively:
I had looked away from him and gazed first at one, then
the other. To their friend's "Is it true or isn't it?" Boldini had replied with a solemn nod while, embarrassed,
he stared at his clasped hands on the table. As for Grassi,
bent as if crushed over his notebook, where he was drawing a caricature, he seemed not even to have heard; but
his silence meant the same thing: namely, that he agreed,
that things were as Cattolica described them. The two of
them were quite different, I thought, from the way I
had always seen them at school. Boldini's hair, for example, wasn't blond at all, but reddish. And the physical
strength that Cattolica attributed to him—a detail to
which I had never *really* paid attention—seemed evident
only now, as I looked at his hands, firmly knotted together, as if to make a single, enormous fist. And Grassi?
Grassi, too, was different. Cattolica had compared him
to Silvio Pellico. An apt comparison. Absorbed in the
drawing of his caricature, he stuck out the tip of his
tongue from time to time and left it there, gray, at the
corner of his mouth. Apt. The comparison struck home.

Suddenly I got up, I went to the window, putting my
forehead to the panes. Having vanished a few seconds
before behind the sugar refinery opposite the station, the
sun was no longer irksome, and the view of the space, all
vegetable gardens and flower beds, that stretched from
the Cattolica house to the city walls, and then, beyond,
the endless plain, suddenly made me want to be there,
outside, with those little boys on the top of the bastions,
chasing a ball, or else over there, on the local train that

slowly, its windows open, was leaving the station at that very moment, or there in the distance, along the fine paved road to Pontelagoscuro, on the little yellow trolley, tiny as a tin can, teetering off toward the black line of the Po's right bank. Now it must be growing cooler outside, I said to myself, and if not today, then tomorrow evening surely, at this same hour (tomorrow evening at this hour *everything* would have been long finished!), I would take my bike and be off, I would go by myself to see the Po. The Po in full flood. And alone, finally, after having unmasked Luciano, after having broken with him, yes, but also with all the others: alone, forever.

"What a wretch!" Cattolica repeated. "When I think there are people like Pulga in this world, it makes my blood boil."

I turned. I couldn't wait until it was over.

"Will he really come?" I asked, looking at him, I think, with hatred.

"Don't worry. To pry his way into other people's houses, he would walk for miles, that one, with those toothpick legs of his. You know how certain mongrels are? You just have to whistle and they come trotting up, wagging their tail. That's Pulga. A real mongrel. Dying to force his way inside, you understand? And not because he really needs something. It's simply a question of character"—and he was also referring to me, now, he was also covertly insulting me. "Look, maybe it's because I'm not a bastard and not a mongrel, either, and to tell you the truth, I can't stand them, they give me goose flesh, I'm only happy in my own house, whereas, on the contrary, there are people in this world who can't stand their own homes. . . ."

"What time did you tell him to come?"

He looked at his handsome chrome wristwatch, an Eberhard, and pursed his lips.

"There's time yet. I told him, and I repeated it, that he wasn't to show up before seven, and since he's obedient we have a good twenty-five minutes to work things out."

Even though he had spoken of a "plan to make him talk," I had got it into my head, for some reason, that he had prepared a kind of trial for Luciano, with himself, Cattolica, acting as judge; Boldini and Grassi as jury, witnesses, and police; while the two of us, Luciano and I, would argue before the court. I had imagined, basically, a direct confrontation; and during the last few hours it had been this prospect, of a face-to-face meeting, that had gradually gripped my stomach more and more oppressively in a vise of anguish. So I felt real relief when I learned from Cattolica that his famous plan did not involve my presence in the room at all, and therefore no "scene." At Luciano's arrival I would move into the next room (saying this, Cattolica nodded toward a door, which I hadn't noticed, behind Boldini), from which, unseen, I could hear with the greatest convenience everything "the creature," cleverly questioned, would surely start saying about me again. I wasn't to move. I was only to listen, that's all, leaving the three of them to do the rest. But meanwhile, would I please go for a moment in there, into the room in question (it was his parents' bedroom), taking care to leave the door ajar? It was necessary, I was to trust him; I could realize, in advance, how I would be able to hear.

Not to see him, Luciano! Not to be forced to look him

in the face while Cattolica made him talk! Overwhelmed
by a sudden euphoria, I didn't have to be asked twice;
moving from the window, I passed behind Boldini and
slipped into the adjoining room.

It was dark in there, or at least so it seemed to me:
a deep, basement darkness. I stood by the door, my eyes
fixed on the crack.

I said gaily: "Talk! Go ahead and talk!"

"You see, Gianni," Cattolica began saying, calmly,
to Boldini, "I simply don't believe it's a matter of . . ."

"That's right," the other boy answered. "Yes, that's
it. . . ."

"Can you hear us?" Cattolica asked, raising his
voice.

"Perfectly!" I shouted. "I can hear you perfectly!"

And I came back into the study.

I sat down again, but now they no longer knew what
to say. Grassi had gone back to his drawing; Boldini was
looking outside, apparently attracted by the little flap-
ping black rags, bats, at times so close to the window
that they seemed about to slam against it. Dusk was falling. Cattolica was silent, too. He glanced at his watch
again.

"What time is it?" I asked.

"Another ten minutes."

He shook his head, as if dissatisfied. I asked him if
by chance there was something wrong, and he denied it,
sadly. I insisted, and then he admitted that yes, in fact,
there was something wrong.

"Maybe we're making a great mistake," he said.

He added, then, staring at me, that if, after having
allowed Pulga to talk his fill, I wanted to come out of my

hiding place and then and there give him the punishment he deserved, namely, a sound beating, I shouldn't hesitate; none of them would lift a finger to prevent me. On the contrary.

"What!" I exclaimed. "Here?"

"Why not? Delayed punishment almost amounts to forgiveness. Let's suppose that tomorrow morning, at school, you take him aside and begin saying to him: 'See here, Luciano . . . ,'" and he began to speak nasally, in a saccharine tone, as if this were the tone Luciano and I customarily used in our talk. "'. . . See here, Luciano, yesterday evening, at Cattolica's, I was also present, hidden behind a door.' Well, if you start talking to him like that, you're done for, my friend. Liar and cheat that he is, Pulga would be able to convince you, no doubt, that he didn't mean it, that you misunderstood, and so on. He might even be capable of getting mad— why not?—and saying these things aren't done, that a friend never sets such a trap for a friend, and that he, anyway, catching on to the snare at once, said bad things about you on purpose, just to punish your treachery. . . . I can almost see the two of you," he laughed. "And the whole thing, as always, would end in a puff of smoke."

He was right. I, too, could see myself and Luciano; and then, a little later, Luciano again at my house, to do his homework. As if nothing had happened. Nothing at all.

"All right," I said, uncertainly, looking around. "But how can we do it, in here?"

Cattolica sprang to his feet. "I'll prepare the ring for you!"

In a flash, by himself, he dragged the leather sofa and the little table beneath the side window, then, to the other side, against one of the bookcases, the armchairs. He quickly rolled back the central rug and hid it under the bed.

"There," he said, straightening up, all flushed, coming back toward us.

From the other side of the table, Boldini stared at me with his blue eyes, the same icy blue, I noticed, as Luciano's. Neither he nor Grassi had ever been talkative types, with others. If they did talk, it was among themselves, and with Cattolica; but whispering intently, like seminarians, and ready, in any case, as soon as some outsider approached them, to leave Cattolica to do the talking for them too.

Now Boldini looked me straight in the eye, and this in itself was unusual. Then he tightened his mouth, as if to repress a tremor of shyness, and asked me, gravely, raising his pointed chin: "You aren't afraid, are you?"

"Afraid!" I laughed. "What an idea!"

But he didn't seem very convinced. He began asking me how much I weighed; then he wanted to know how much I thought Luciano might weigh; concluding, finally, that in his opinion it would take me only one slap, "well placed," to put him "on the canvas."

He stood up, passed behind Grassi, and came to test the muscles of my right arm, and at the same time (quiet for once, Cattolica merely nodded) he went on reassuring me about the outcome of the imminent match, which, he was sure, would end rapidly in my favor with a K.O., and he gave me advice about how to hit. I was to aim at the stomach, he said, with my left, and then at once "follow through" with a quick right to the chin. It was easy, he guaranteed—nothing to it.

"Come here and I'll show you."

I followed him into the center of the room, into the ring arranged by Cattolica. And we were still there, beneath the dazed eyes of Cattolica and Grassi, one of us facing the other, like boxing instructor and pupil, carefully rehearsing again and again the "tactics," as he said, when we heard the doorbell.

XI

A little earlier, in the brief time I had stayed there, the bedroom of Cattolica's parents had seemed plunged in total darkness. But it wasn't. I had only to enter again (as before, I leaned against the wall, beside the slightly opened door), and in a few seconds I realized I had been mistaken: there was a light.

In the bigger room, they had already turned on the table lamp. Its light, stealing through the open crack of the door, was a white strip that, at my feet, sharply cut the floor of dark, hexagonal tiles, identical to those of the ground floor. Before it reached the opposite wall and then scaled it, to the ceiling, the shaft of light encountered no object in its path. The dim glow, like a crypt's, which spread through the room—not large, for that matter, not half the size of the study—came chiefly from a little quarter-watt bulb, burning beneath a holy picture in the center of the wall on my right. Alone, the light was enough to pick out not only the picture itself (a Jesus with languid blue eyes, blond hair carefully parted in the middle, coral lips with a hint of two white teeth, and a feminine, alabaster hand limply raised to point at a large, red heart stuck, like a fruit, at the top of his chest) but also the parallel outlines, below, of two beds, side by side and separate, massive as tombstones, and in the background, as if to keep vigil over them, the blackish hulks of a dresser and a wardrobe.

I was tense, alert, but calm. I stared at that excessive red heart, in the image of Jesus, and my own heart, which at first had been pounding in my throat, grew quieter. I was no longer there, for that matter, a few feet from the voices of Cattolica and Luciano, who, after slowly climbing the stairs, were still lingering, chatting on the landing. No, I was no longer there. The room that hid me suddenly assumed the guise of an infinitely more secret, remote, even more tenebrous place than it really was: a spot, lost in an immense space, vast as the ocean. . . .

Once they were all seated around the table, with Luciano, I guessed, in the place I had occupied until a moment before, when and how would they come to talk about me?

They had two hours before them; and perhaps also for this reason, besides the pleasure he surely felt at keeping me on tenterhooks, Cattolica made no effort to rush things. He listened. Patient and crafty as a cat with a mouse, he listened to the mouse, as he droned on and on, with his typical Bolognese loquacity. He talked, Pulga did, about trivial matters; he, too, was evading. Well, then? Cattolica seemed to want to say, remaining almost always silent. Well then? Let the little swine run on, let him do his best to seem amusing and interesting, to repay as best he could the priceless gift of having been received here where he now was. Sooner or later (from the tone of his rare answers, his measured replies to the steady buzz of Luciano's voice, I realized how sure of himself Cattolica felt) he would do with him exactly what all of us, including me, had agreed to do with him.

For a long time, then, for a good half-hour, Luciano said only things that concerned me indirectly, if they concerned me at all.

He began with his homework, of all things. He asked if they had finished. And when Cattolica answered yes, they had just finished, only a moment before he arrived, Luciano sighed: they were lucky, all right! He, on the contrary, had managed to scribble only a part, the Latin and the Italian, but he hadn't done the Greek assignment yet. No, no thanks, really! he exclaimed then—and I could literally *see* the sharp, sideways shift of his jaw— it wasn't necessary for him, for Cattolica, to lend him his notebook. To translate the ninety-eight verses of the *Iliad*, assigned by "that bastard" Guzzo, he had the whole evening, after supper, and the early hours of the morning, apart from the fact that, for once, he would rather do it on his own. He wanted that very much, he repeated firmly, especially since, if he took advantage of Cattolica's kind offer, it might seem he had come here just for that, whereas he had simply come to have a quiet little chat.

From homework he went on to philosophy.

Razzetti still had to question him in class, he said, so tomorrow morning, when he had finished with the *Iliad*, he meant to take a quick look also at the *Phaedo*, you never can tell. . . . Razzetti, of course, was not really a philosophy scholar; he had been teaching the subject only since the Gentile Scholastic Reforms had been in effect, proceeding, as he also did with history, with the help of the usual synopses and study plans. Still, wasn't Plato himself almost as tiresome as poor old Razzetti? Wasn't the *Phaedo* a pack of nonsense? And Socrates! With that smug manner of his all the time, Professor Know-It-All, and instead what an idiot he was, what a fool! Thank goodness in the end (he had read ahead) they actually gave him the "proverbial" hemlock, which was the only way they had of shutting him up, after all, that presumptuous pain in the ass. . . . But even forgetting about Plato and Socrates, philosophy itself, in his modest opinion, was all balls. And they needn't try to tell him they believed in it.

"What do you mean?" Cattolica answered. "Philosophy isn't religion, after all. You don't have to believe in it!"

"Forgive my ignorance, but what is it, then?"

Slowly, with kind tolerance, Cattolica began to expound his own opinions on the subject of philosophy, and Grassi also spoke up from time to time, and even Boldini.

"Maybe you're right," Luciano admitted at a certain point.

Meanwhile, however, he added, with his memory in such bad shape "after beating the meat all the time," God knows what bad marks he would get, the next morning, if Razzetti really did decide to call on him. With the scant intelligence he knew he had, with his memory reduced to a flicker (he wasn't Cattolica, unfortunately, who had to read something only once!), would they please, Boldini and Grassi, in the first desk, try to prompt him?

But to get back to the *Phaedo:* as he had already said, it seemed to him, beyond any doubt, nothing but talk,

talk, talk. Still, there was one theory in it, in the *Phaedo*, he had to admit, which, though it was probably nonsense, too, had pretty much convinced him.

"I bet it's the theory of metempsychosis," Cattolica said.

"How did you guess?" Luciano asked, amazed. "Yes, that's the one."

Cattolica answered that if there was one thing in the *Phaedo* in which he did *not* believe, it was precisely the theory of the transmigration of the souls of men into animals and vice versa. To believe that, you would have to throw the Catholic religion out the window. And he, as a good Catholic, believed in Heaven, Purgatory, and Hell.

"I won't argue with you about it," Luciano answered, primly. "Still, I *feel* that there is some truth in metempsychosis."

If Cattolica would just listen a moment. Guzzo, for example, he began by saying, before being born with two legs and two arms, had probably been a poisonous snake: a viper or a cobra, take your choice; and he would go back to that form, God willing, the moment he had kicked the bucket. La Krauss, perched up in her laboratory among her retorts and alembics, gave herself airs like some kind of wise owl, but more likely she came from a duck: you only had to look at her behind. With Half-Pint, it was hard to say: he had probably been an earthworm, the kind you see by the handful, in the country, if you kick a clod, tiny, of course, but nice and fat and pink.

Then, coming down to our classmates: Mazzanti had most probably been a rat, it was only a question of what kind, house or barn or sewer. Chieregatti, a mule; Lattuga, a pig, naturally, or perhaps even a hyena, since hyenas eat carrion, corpses from cemeteries, and stink even worse than pigs. Donadio, a guinea pig. Camurri, a mole. Droghetti, with that nose of his, a dromedary; Selmi, a horse, a hack, that is. Veronesi and Danieli, poor things, two jackasses, the kind with their "things" always swaying. And so on. Now, assuming for a moment that metempsychosis wasn't the balls that maybe it was, they would all return, in time, to their original forms; except for Lattuga, who in all likelihood would be reborn a worm, the kind that "wallow" in people's intestines "up to their knees in shit"; and except for Mazzanti, who, instead of being reborn a rat, even a sewer rat, might find himself a louse, picking his way through somebody's pubic hair.

"You've left out the girls," Cattolica remarked.

"They don't count. Have you ever taken a good look at them? Where could they come from? They were all geese and hens."

I heard him snicker, excited and pleased with himself.

"What about me?" Cattolica insisted. "Where might I come from, in your opinion? Go ahead, tell me."

"Well, you might come from a bird, too: a falcon, one of those big ones, the Alpine falcons, or from a hawk, or even from an eagle. *'Who above all others,'*" he declaimed, in a nasal tone, " *'like an eagle soars. . . .'*"

"Aha! And Boldini?"

"Wait a minute. He may have been a jaguar, or a sea elephant. And you, Grassi, you know who you were? A beaver. That's it. One of those little animals with two huge front teeth, always in the water, building dams. . . ."

In every instance, he went on, he, like Plato, believed that there must be few, *very* few men and women who, on being reborn, managed not to regress. He himself perhaps had been a dog (certain days he could feel it, in his skin). And so it was almost mathematically certain that in the future he would "go back to that starting line," unless, like Mazzanti and Lattuga, he fell even further down.

For a few seconds they remained quiet, perfectly silent.

"So, to sum up," Cattolica resumed finally—and at that moment I thought I heard a little sound, as if he had struck a match—"Lattuga a tapeworm, Mazzanti a louse, and you?"

"Hm," he answered. "We'll see."

He then said that if he had been allowed to choose the type of parasite in which to be reincarnated, he would almost have preferred to drop to the very bottom of the scale, and instead of a flea or a louse, he would rather be reborn as a germ, that's it, a germ! No worries about eating and drinking . . . guaranteed invisibility to the naked eye . . . the fat of the land, in other words. Responsibilities? You only had to be rather modest: first of all, avoid imitating those germs, like the typhoid germ, or, say, that of rabies or tetanus or pneumonia, who enjoy, or rather delight in, destroying the whole works in a few days. On the contrary, the thing was to imitate the smarter germs, the kind who find a quiet little place and stay there peacefully sucking for twenty, thirty, forty years, and in the final analysis don't bother anybody much. The syphilis bacillus, or tuberculosis (tuberculosis of the bone, in any case, or of the glands): these were the bright "characters," able to live and let live! His father always said the same.

He snickered again, alone. The others were holding their breath.

It was then, at this point, that Cattolica pronounced my name (it didn't sound like mine, as if it belonged to a stranger). Very well, I heard him say, assuming for the sake of argument that he, Pulga, had been a dog, what had I been, then? What was I?

"He was a dog, too," he answered, without hesitation. "No doubt about it."

With this basic difference between himself and me, in any case, he added that while he had been, he was ready to swear, one of those "pooches," small and of no financial value, the result of love-making among countless breeds, always wandering the streets looking for things to sniff and impartially curious about every turd or pee stain, I, on the contrary, must have been a big dog, not a purebred, of course, but still a fairly good cross (an Alsatian father and a setter mother, or a pointer mother and a mastiff father, or something of the sort), the kind that makes a good showing in whatever situation and therefore easily finds a family to settle with permanently and grow fat. To sum up: a big but not enormous dog, nice-looking but not really handsome, sturdy but not strong, energetic but not actually courageous, the sort that when it runs into a little mongrel "of the Pulga variety," for example (weighing maybe four pounds, and a hand or two high), one way or another, ends up being led by the mongrel, wherever it chooses. And they mustn't think that it's the "big dog" that keeps its nose under the other's tail all the time. No, indeed. Quite the contrary!

XII

When they had finished laughing (they had all four burst out laughing: Luciano laughed, Boldini and Grassi laughed, even Cattolica laughed), they began again. Now they were talking about me, only me. And, as before, the voices of Luciano and Cattolica prevailed over the voices of the other two.

What did they say?

Cattolica was asking Luciano how he had managed to break the appointment he had made with me earlier. And Luciano answered that it was simple, everything had gone smooth as silk, since I had been the one—yes, I—to announce, first, that I wasn't free that afternoon. Of course, he said, when I had taken the initiative from him, sparing him the trouble of inventing some story, he had been overjoyed. He had been a little less pleased, all the same, that I had left him completely at sea, without considering the fact that he, no longer accustomed to studying alone, would have to sweat blood to get by. What a way to act! he exclaimed; when a person has got used to a certain arrangement, afterward he relies on it, that's obvious. But instead . . . With me, however, it had been useless. He had insisted, in vain, trying to move as far forward as possible our usual afternoon meeting.

It was no use at all: I wouldn't hear of it. I said my throat hurt, and for this reason I had to go to an uncle, a doctor. But it was an excuse, probably.

"An excuse?" Cattolica said, his voice betraying not the slightest trepidation. "Why would he need an excuse?"

"Who knows? It's not easy to understand him. He seems naïve, and he *is* naïve. But he's also so complicated, you've no idea, so suspicious and devious. He takes offense at the least little thing!"

Unfortunately, he went on, between the three of them and me there was some hostility, no use denying that; so he, too, worse luck, had had to suffer the consequences of the situation. But by the way, what had *really* happened, between us, to make me so bitter against them, and against him, Cattolica, especially? What had they done to me, *really*? He knew by experience the sort of quirks you could expect from a Jew. But I was so angry! What had happened?

"I'm amazed," Cattolica answered calmly. "Personally, I've never had anything against him. Quite the contrary. And neither have the two of them."

"You know what I think?"

"What?"

"I think," Luciano went on, lowering his voice, "he's bitter chiefly because he was dying to be your friend . . . maybe to come here, to your house, and study with you. And instead," he laughed, "he never made it."

"No, no, where did you get that idea?" Cattolica said, with a hint of impatience. "In the first place, we're very good friends; otherwise, tell me, why would we go on sitting together for so many months, at the same desk?

And secondly," he continued, also lowering his voice, "if, as you say, he wanted to come here so badly, to study at my house, why didn't he ever ask me? He could easily have asked me, don't you think?"

"Of course he could have!" Luciano exclaimed. "But, if I may say so (I'm trying to put myself in his shoes), if he'd been the one to ask you such a thing, what satisfaction would he have got out of it? You see, he wanted—and I know the type, I know what I'm saying— he wanted, not so much to come here, as to be invited here. And since you never gave that idea a thought, that's why he's so against you, secretly."

There was the sound of a shifted chair, and I realized Cattolica had stood up. His footsteps, first muffled by the carpets, suddenly rang out on the bared wood of the "ring," then died away again. Perhaps he had gone to sit on the bed, I surmised, at the end of the room. Or else to lie down on it.

"But what about you?" he said finally, from over there, "what had he done to you, to make you speak against him all the time? You should really be his friend, after all! Why is it that, instead, you can't bear him?"

Luciano also rose from his chair. Probably he felt a need to move closer to Cattolica, and, in fact, when he answered, his voice sounded different, farther away.

He said it was true, in fact, that he couldn't stand me. But not so much because I was unpleasant or because, as he had said other times, I had acted badly toward him. Oh, no, he exclaimed—he criticized me for reasons much more serious than a mere incompatibility of character, which did indeed exist but was of only minor importance. And he wasn't acting from any trivial resentment, like some hysterical adolescent. He was sufficiently superior, for his part, sufficiently calm not to indulge in reactions of that sort in any case. But for this very reason, precisely because he felt superior to all pettiness, not even gratitude—on which I, however, was clearly counting—would prevent him from looking squarely at reality and saying about me, objectively, everything he felt it was appropriate and useful to say.

My vanity, my incredible, absurd vanity, like a small child's—that, in the first place, was something he couldn't swallow.

He had noticed it at once, from the very beginning: that is to say, when he set foot in my house for the first time.

"Have you ever been to his house?" he asked.

"No," Cattolica answered, "I never go to other people's houses on principle."

Now, Luciano went on, no question about it: it was, beyond any doubt, a real palazzo, big, like four or five modern houses put together (modern houses like this one, Cattolica's, or like the one where they lived, beyond Porta Reno), and, what's more, with a magnificent garden. And, besides, my family, which had taken the whole third floor for itself, occupied by itself an apartment of something like twenty rooms, which must have cost God knows what to heat in the winter. We were loaded with money, in other words, and you could see it. Still, a gentleman's a gentleman, and the nouveau riche are something else again. And I myself had confirmed the fact that our money dated back no further than my paternal grandfather, a wholesale cloth merchant; I had told him that first day when, without even giving him time to catch his breath, I had taken him all around from room to room. I had shown him everything, *at once*: the ballroom, the three living rooms, the two dining rooms, the seven bedrooms, the four baths, the kitchen, the pantry, and even the toilets, the servants' toilets; and I was ecstatic, the whole time, so smug it was disgusting. How was it possible to be so vain, so deeply pompous, for God's sake? Over all the doors of the apartment, my grandfather, who apparently was very religious, had hung up some old circles of shiny metal the size of a five-centesimi piece, with a scroll inside written in "Jewish." He had asked me to explain; and you ought to have seen me, as I expounded, in complete detail, the meaning and the function of these gadgets, my face red with pleasure! What was written in those disks? Why, nothing! The name of our God, that's all. But I was so vain, obviously, that even religion was transformed, for me, into a source of family pride. Our God, I had told him, was the father of Jesus Christ, the Eternal Father and no one else (Christianity, in my view, was merely a more modern form of Judaism). All well and good. But I talked about him, about my "old man with a beard," with the same familiarity, the same ridiculous boasting that I might have used in speaking of my cloth-merchant grandfather, rest his soul. . . .

Then we had started studying together, every day. But here, too, I felt such obvious delight in showing off, in standing out (everything, for me, was a reason for competition: at home as at school I always behaved as if I were playing football), that anyone with me could feel only one desire: to let me go ahead, let me do it all, if that was what I longed for, and let it go at that. True, "scholastically speaking," he had, in a way, lived off me for some months, transformed by me into a kind of leech. But after all! A leech is a poor invertebrate, whom you can rightly expect "to thank you for squashing him"; whereas a schoolmate, even if his family is less rich, even if he is less intelligent and less well-prepared, even if he isn't at all displeased, finally, to find someone who does all the work for him, he's still a schoolmate, a human being! I had never considered him a human being, still less a friend, that was the truth. He was simply a flattery machine, to be operated, at will, as idly and casually as you might turn a knob and start the shower in your bathroom.

He had almost never seen my brother and sister, who, anyway, were of no importance: the boy was still in the second year of Ginnasio, and the other, the little girl, in the third grade of elementary school. But my parents, yes, he had had the opportunity of seeing them often, especially my mother. And he felt that my mother always treated him in the same way, as something useful, something that might come in handy (for various uses, even . . .).

"His mother?" Cattolica asked, in the tomblike silence that followed Luciano's last words.

I heard him cross the room, passing the slightly opened door, and sit at the table again.

"What do you mean?" he went on, in a low, upset, but close-sounding voice. "Come. Make yourself clear. I don't understand."

"Of course," Luciano went on, after a brief pause; and his voice, too, was now close. "Haven't you ever seen her?"

"No."

"Well, too bad, because, as women go, I can assure you she's worth looking at."

He then began his description.

She was a lady of about thirty-four, thirty-five, he said, maybe "going to seed a bit," especially the breasts, maybe a little stout, like all Jewesses; but with a mouth, my friend, and with a pair of brown eyes and a look in them, especially, which promises, "in bed, God only knows what." (As for my father, he digressed, he was nothing. Once he had received his own father, making a disastrous impression on him, too. Lots of airs, like a great gentleman, always turning up his nose. He didn't do a thing from morning to night, the lucky man, because, though he was a doctor, he didn't practice. His only occupation was spending his afternoons at the Club. What a life! But you could understand. With a wife like that, it was a miracle if he had enough breath left in him, during the day, to hold a hand of cards. . . .)

My mother and I, though she had dark hair and eyes, were as alike as two drops of water, in every way. Just as I, vain and requiring praise, used him, Luciano, the way you use a trapeze, to measure the strength of my muscles, similarly, my mother had constantly exploited him, as a stratagem, the best way to keep me, her smart little boy, always calmly at home until evening. She would have gone to any lengths, the worthy lady, to achieve her noble ends. She would have done anything, he was willing to swear it. She arrived at five o'clock with trays so laden that a whole family, a normal family, could have been amply fed for two days. Coffee, tea, chocolate, whipped cream, cake, pastries, petit-fours, candies: the whole array every afternoon. But that was nothing! Because apart from her manner, "damn her," when she filled your cup or held the plate of cookies under your nose ("Do help yourself, don't be shy," she would urge, insinuatingly: "Sweets are good for you, they make muscle and brain cells!"), she never forgot, afterward, saying good-by, to fire from the open door a beautiful smile with a glance "partly maternal and partly tormenting, that's right, a real torment!" And the kisses that she often pressed on her son's cheek, only a couple of feet away, all tender, it seemed, at finding him there, in the warmth of the radiators, so studious and handsome and intelligent, what about those kisses?

One evening this past winter, one stormy evening, she had gone even further. To persuade him to stay for supper, and perhaps to sleep there, she had taken to staring at him for a while, looking him straight in the eye, with such insistence (as if to hint: "Stay, you fool, and you'll have a good time!") that she would have frightened not only him, which didn't take much, but the devil himself. With that look, what was she promising, *really*? No, that was enough of that. But one sure thing: a woman like her, in the summer, at the shore (we would be going to Cesenatico the following summer, don't forget!), must have played all sorts of tricks on her elderly husband, during the weeks when she was alone in the villa with only the children and the maids! With that wide, "greedy" mouth, with those languid eyes half hidden by her hair (her breasts sagged a bit, to be sure, but the "rest," in a bathing suit, was worth making a special trip, just to see), it was *impossible* that when an opportunity arose, she would let it slip by.

But to get back to me: would they believe that I didn't even know what jerking off meant? He suspected as much, to tell the truth, he had always suspected it. But nevertheless the day when, with my back to the wall, I had confessed it, he had been so surprised he could hardly believe his ears. At the age of sixteen! And with all my pretensions!

Later, after a lot of insistence, he had made me show him my "pistol," which, although "shorn" permanently by my circumcision, had seemed "completely normal" to him. But there had been something else, on the other hand, which he considered "pretty significant": my reaction when he, a moment before, to persuade me to unbutton my pants, had shown me his own "thing."

Well, I had gone so pale, on seeing it, and then, in the days after that, my behavior had been so changed (I had suddenly become rude, curt, I even avoided looking him in the face, as if he disgusted me, or—who knows?—made me angry or afraid) that he inevitably had been led to think the worst about me. Of course, I was surely a "pansy," though still only potentially; a "fairy," only waiting to become one, to become one really, and at the same time unaware—that was the tragic thing!—of the fine career that was before me, inevitably. . . .

XIII

On tiptoe, slowly emerging from the shadows into the light, I approached the large glass door that separated the living room from the dining room.

It was long after nine, and my family, as I had foreseen, were already at supper. Through the glass I could see my mother, seated with her back to me, wearing a light summer dress, white, her shoulders, neck, and arms bare. Opposite her were the others: my father, my brother Ernesto at his right, and Fanny, at the head of the table, on his left. But not even the faces of my father and my brother and sister (I could no longer remember my mother's face, invisible), brightly lighted by the lamp over the rectangular table, seemed the same to me now, the familiar, unjudged and unjudgeable faces of every day, of always. Who were they, all of them? I wondered, looking at them. Was my father that man with the graying hair, with the signs of premature old age on his thin, haggard face, who, in his pajama jacket and slippers, was finishing a bowl of soup? Were my brother and sister those two insignificant children, eating, serious and proper, but, you could tell, ready to burst into loud laughter at any moment? Was my mother the handsome lady with her back to me, her hair haloed by light, and her left hand, when she stretched it beyond the dark, soft curve of her shoulder toward the center of the table, with rings glistening on the fingers? And was it possible that I, I too, was the son of that mediocre man, bored and boring, unable, especially at home, to assume authority to keep his end up, and of that woman, so vulgar, after all, with her low-cut dresses and her rings ("um-pa, um-pa": were they, too, like that? In bed, obscenely, vilely naked?), and did I owe to that union, to that physical union, my own existence?

The maid came in, with the dishes of meat and vegetables, and immediately, from the surprised and almost frightened expression on her face, I realized I had been discovered.

"Oh, here he is!" she cried.

There was nothing to be done. I lowered the handle of the glass door, advancing amid general silence toward the table.

I sat at my place, next to my mother.

"But, darling, it's half past nine!" she said. "Where have you been?"

She examined my face, my hands, my clothes, everything: as if to make sure, rapidly, that I was still whole. And from that glance of hers, shy, concerned, and at the same time, cunning, guilty; motherly, yes, but no longer only motherly (the first of those motherly and womanly glances with which she was to greet me so many other times, in later years, whenever I came home after an absence, perhaps of days); from it I suddenly sensed how, in the terrible wound that had been inflicted on me a little earlier, so brutal, sudden, and definitive, she also shared. Who knows? In a mysterious way perhaps she had felt it at the same moment I had.

"I was at a friend's house," I answered, staring at my empty bowl.

"Cattolica's?"

"Yes."

"The new flame, eh? And what about Pulga? What does he have to say? Was he there, too?"

"What a way to behave!" my father interrupted, raising his voice indignantly. "You could have telephoned, it seems to me. That would have been a simple thing to do."

"Yes, Pulga was there, too," I murmured, gravely, not looking up.

My father opened his mouth to go on scolding me, but my mother promptly, with a gesture of her beringed hand, silenced him.

"Would you like some cold soup?" she asked me.

I nodded.

But I wasn't hungry. I ate slowly, my spoon half full, feeling my stomach reject the food. I saw myself again in the bedroom of Cattolica's parents, my back to the wall, staring at the Jesus with the red heart, and I could hear again the calm, tireless buzz of Luciano's voice through the wall. No, I hadn't gone out, I hadn't appeared. When Luciano said, laughing: "It's all very well for him to slave away at Latin, Greek, and all the rest! What career can he have, after all, except that?" Then, finally, stirring, I had moved from the wall, slowly crossed the room, and gone out onto the landing. In the deep darkness (Luciano's voice continued its buzz, beyond; he showed no sign of wanting to stop) I went down the steps, found my bicycle in the pantry, and then outside, in the air, in the darkness, different but no less deep, of Via Cittadella, pedaling, my head down, faster and faster. Viale Cavour, Corso Giovecca, on and on, never turning back, as if in a dark tunnel, straight and endless . . .

"Aren't you hungry, darling?" my mother asked.

I shook my head.

"He probably had something to eat," my father said.

I stood up, pushing back the leather chair with my legs.

"My stomach's a little upset," I said. "I'd better skip supper."

"What did you eat?" my father insisted. "Ice cream?"

"I didn't eat a damn thing," I answered, staring hard into his eyes, with hatred.

"Calm down there," he said, intimidated. "In a bad humor, eh?"

"Good night," I said.

And without giving him or my mother the usual good-night kiss on the cheek, I quickly left the room.

As soon as I was in my own room, I undressed, stretched out on the bed, turned off the light, and immediately grasped my member. But I was limp, as if dead. I kept trying. Nothing happened.

Bathed in sweat, I was about to begin again, when, in the hall, I heard my mother's footsteps.

She stopped at the door, obviously uncertain what to do. I heard her call me in a low, hollow voice, then the room, after a slight creak of the door, was filled with her presence. What did she want of me? I thought angrily, my eyes shut, as I pretended to sleep. I sensed her near the bed, tall and silent over my outstretched body, and I would have liked to stand up, insult her, hit her, drive her away. Instead, delicate, cool and delicate as ever, her hand came down in the darkness to touch my forehead and rest there. And that simple contact was enough, suddenly, to restore my calm, as I prepared, a little later, alone again, to sink once more into my old, restoring, childhood sleep.

The next morning, coming into the classroom, I immediately saw that they were all there, each already seated in his place. Luciano was prompt to greet me with a smile and a gay wave. But from the attitude of Boldini and Grassi, bent over a notebook held between them, and apparently entirely absorbed in it, and from Cattolica's manner especially, whose gaze, as I approached, never left me for a moment, it was clear that they also realized the irreparable seriousness of what had happened the previous evening. Cattolica waited until I sat down and didn't even greet me; he simply smiled at me, uncertainly moving his lips. He was bewildered and anxious. But anxious, why? What was it that kept him in suspense, I wondered. Was it perhaps the hope that I hadn't stayed till the end and, therefore, hadn't heard the worst? Perhaps. In any case, if his hope was only that, before the morning was over I would completely undeceive him. Everything was finished, between us, finished forever. And he must know it, too, as soon as possible.

"You were right to leave," he said, in fact, a little later, covering his mouth with his hand. "I promise you, it was absolutely not worth your staying."

I nodded, in ironic agreement, and didn't answer.

He sighed.

"He's mad," he went on, after a long pause. "A poor lunatic."

"Skip it, and don't bother me," I said coldly, without turning to look at him.

There was Guzzo, seated up at his desk. At the very moment I spoke these words, not bothering to hide my mouth, I noticed the professor was observing me.

"Beginning again, are we?" he said, threateningly.

Quickly, as if inspired, I sprang to my feet and looked firmly into his eyes.

"Please, sir," I said. "I'd like to ask you to change my seat."

"And why, if I may inquire?" Guzzo said. "Do you realize, my dear friend, that we're less than ten days from the end of term?"

"I know, sir, I know. But that's why I want to change. Here, with him," I went on, nodding toward Cattolica, immobile at my side, "we're always distracting each other."

My words were received with a long whispering of amazement and disapproval.

"May I ask the class to maintain strict silence?" Guzzo shouted.

He couldn't believe his eyes or his ears. But there I was, standing, erect and inflexible, determined to obtain what I had requested.

He looked around, searching for a desk.

"To which desk would you like to move?" he asked, with a hint of respect in his voice. "There don't seem to be any empty ones."

"I'd like to go back there," I said, pointing at Luciano's desk, without turning around. "To the desk where Pulga is. But alone."

"And what about *Signor* Pulga?"

"Pulga could come here perfectly well."

"Ah, you're suggesting a double transfer!" Guzzo exclaimed, amused. *"Do ut des . . .* Very well, then. Permission granted. *Fiat.* You understand, Pulga Luciano? Come on, hurry, collect your possessions, and advance. To the fourth desk, beside the great Cattolica. You must feel honored, I imagine!"

And as Luciano, laden with his books, passed me in the aisle between the second and third rows of desks (as he grazed by me, he gave me an amazed, frightened look), a sharp "ssssh," hissing and imperious, was heard, to kill at birth a new murmur in the room.

To regain the total solitude of the previous autumn, I still had to take the final step: I had to break with Luciano.

Still, at noon, after the *finis* bell, when I glimpsed him, walking all alone in front of me, along the left-hand sidewalk of Via Borgoleoni, pathetically crooked, weighed down by the pack of books he held against his scrawny hip, I had a moment's hesitation. True, in class that morning, every time he had tried to approach me I had treated him with a coldness and a harshness already eloquent in themselves. And yet, why hadn't he waited for me, now? I thought I could almost deduce, from his rapid pace, from the quick precision with which he put one foot in front of the other, that he had guessed everything and was fleeing. My heart pounded painfully in my chest. But if that was so, I thought, displeased with myself, contemptuous of myself, so much the better.

"Hey!" I shouted. "Stop!"

He stopped at once, turning his head. He was very calm, the corners of his thin lips were bent in a smile filled with slightly saddened benevolence.

"Ah, it's you," he said.

We walked on together. He said nothing to me, reproached me for nothing; and this again disconcerted me. At the corner of Corso Giovecca I firmly crossed the street, leaving him a few yards behind.

"What are you doing?" he asked, amazed, when he joined me on the opposite sidewalk. "Aren't you going home?"

"Yes, but I'm bored. I want to change my route. Today I'll accompany you for a bit."

It was a Friday, a market day. Corso Roma and Piazza del Duomo were teeming with the usual rural crowd. We had to force our way ahead, disappearing from each other's view from time to time in the throng, and without exchanging a word. No, he hadn't caught on, I thought, and if I were to allow him, that very afternoon he would turn up at the house again.

At the beginning of Via Porta Reno, just under the clock in the square, I stopped.

"So long," I said.

"So long," he murmured.

He gulped, his Adam's apple bobbed up and down; and at the same time he looked into my eyes. He was pale as a corpse, the down above his lip bathed in sweat.

"Shall we meet later?" he ventured.

"I think not."

"Are you busy?"

I snickered cruelly. "Just my homework."

"What . . . what's wrong?"

"With me? Nothing. What about you?"

His blue eyes widened. "Me?!"

But I had already turned my back on him.

XIV

The very morning when, I knew, the results of the final exams would be displayed in the hall of the Guarini (but I hadn't yet made up my mind to go and look at them), Otello Forti telephoned me.

He had arrived the previous evening, he said; he had finished his orals at five thirty in the afternoon, just in time, then, to go back to the dorm, pack his bags in a rush, and catch the train that left Padua at seven.

I asked him how the exams had gone.

"How did they go?" he said. "Pretty well, I think. What about you? How did you come out?"

I answered that I didn't know, that in fact I was just going to look at the bulletin board.

"Why don't you come by my place on your way?" he suggested. "If you like, we can go together."

He was agreeable, even talkative, with a slight hint of the Veneto in his accent. But not even he meant anything to me any more, and, in any case, I had decided not to be agreeable to anyone from now on.

"You come and pick me up," I said coldly.

He tried to resist. He pointed out that his house was exactly halfway between mine and the Guarini, and therefore it seemed to him more "logical" that I should go to his house. And he was already less pleasant than he had been before, already on his way to becoming again the familiar, tyrannical grumbler, prepared, when he had decided to obtain something, to start the most stubborn arguments.

"Well, listen," I said curtly, bored, "why don't we just meet in front of the Guarini in half an hour? All right?"

"All right, yes, of course," he murmured, taken aback.

Naturally, I had been promoted: with eight in all literary subjects, and only two sixes, one in science and one in physics and mathematics. But where did I stand in the class? First? Second? Third?

It took Otello only one glance (it was eleven thirty, we were alone) in the semidarkness of the entrance hall to calculate that there must be three of us "fighting for first place": me, Cattolica, and Grassi. To be sure, he said, pensively, against my eight in Italian, Cattolica had only a seven to show, and Grassi actually a six. But Cattolica, in mathematics and physics, had an eight, and Grassi in science, a nine. . . .

"You must be second," he concluded, "just one point behind Cattolica. And Grassi must be third, also by a single point."

Extraordinarily considerate and helpful, he took a pencil stub from his pocket and began to write on the wall, beside the board. Luciano, too, had been promoted, I observed, meanwhile; all sixes, but still promoted.

"You see? I was right," Otello announced finally, with a little ring of triumph in his voice. "Cattolica's first, and you're second."

We went outside. I had my bike; he was on foot.

"Aren't you going to call your home?" he asked.

"Why, no. What gave you that idea?" I answered, shrugging. "I'm going there now."

One hand on the seat, and the other on the handlebars, I looked at him. The last time we had spoken to each other, at Christmas, he had seemed suddenly so much taller, so much more adult than I, but now, on the contrary, he seemed smaller, a child.

"You want me to give you a lift to your house?" I suggested. "Climb on."

And, actually, like a child, he obeyed.

Despite the weight, the encumbrance, and the pebbles of the street (to avoid fines from the city police, more numerous along Corso Giovecca, I had preferred to go along the stony Via Mascheraio), I pedaled swiftly. I looked at Otello's nape, so close that beneath his cropped blond hair I could glimpse the pink, fat, tender skin. I could smell the odor of good soap that came from it; and I remembered, in comparison, Luciano's fragile neck, greasy with brilliantine, his big, pale ears, like an old man's, which, seen from behind, were as transparent as membranes. I hadn't given Luciano a ride on my bike more than two or three times; Otello, hundreds. And yet I knew there was nothing for it now: beneath the good, honest odor of Otello—an odor that, for me, was identified with my whole childhood—I would always find also the other, that disgusting and oppressive smell of brilliantine.

As if he also sensed that we would meet only rarely in the future and that, practically speaking, our friendship's minutes were numbered, Otello talked constantly.

He wanted to be brought up to date on a number of things that had happened during these months, while he had been away: with whom I had shared a desk at school, with whom I had studied, with whom I had made friends. And I answered him briefly, mentioned Cattolica, of course, and Luciano, but without telling him anything else. His back was there before me, massive and childish. Speak? Confide in him? In him! I felt as if I were facing a steep, impervious, enormous mountain. The mere idea of having to scale it, such a mountain of obtuseness, was enough to fill me with nausea and impotence.

"Luciano Pulga?" Otello asked. "Who's he? Somebody from out of town?"

"Yes."

"Where's he from?"

"From a mountain village near Bologna. His father's the local doctor at Coronella, but they live here, beyond Porta Reno."

"What's he like? Smart?"

"He gets by."

"Did he pass?"

"Yes, with all sixes."

On the subject of Cattolica, however, I was less laconic. I explained how we had become desk-mates: not because the two of us had sat together, I said, but because of Guzzo, the Classics professor. I added that we had never become real friends.

"Well, as far as being smart goes, he must be all right," Otello remarked at this point. "Did you see all those eights?"

We had arrived. I put on my brake sharply and

dropped one foot to the ground. Getting off the bike, Otello immediately looked into my eyes.

"Come inside for a minute," he said.

"No, I'm sorry, I have to go."

I pressed the pedals hard, then looked back.

"I'll phone you," I shouted, already far away. "Next week we're leaving for the seaside."

At home, my mother was waiting for me. She was seated in the garden, in the shade of the magnolia. As soon as I came in from the street (the sudden passing from the burning heat outside to the airy coolness of the vestibule made me sneeze), I saw her, there in the distance, raising her head. If I were to go to my room by the back stairs, crossing the garden, I thought, I couldn't avoid stopping and talking with her: with her who, for days, I felt, had been keeping a watchful eye on me constantly. Noon had just struck: we had plenty of time. But what would we talk about? If there were two people in the world who had absolutely nothing to say to each other, we were those two people.

I sneezed again, and, to gain time, I took my handkerchief from my pocket and blew my nose. From the center of the vestibule, my bicycle propped against my hip, I looked through half-closed lids at my mother, dressed in white. Immersed in the sun-streaked shade that collected around the trunk of the magnolia, she was no more than a bright, distant spot.

I saw her raise her arm.

"Oo-hoo," she cried, modulating her lovely, singer's voice in her favorite summons.

I disappeared to one side. I put my bicycle in its usual place, beneath the stairs, then reappeared. Instead of going into the garden, however, I stopped at the end of the portico.

"I'm going upstairs a moment to telephone," I said.

"Were you promoted?"

"Yes."

"What sort of marks?"

"I have to make a call," I answered and slipped away.

Upstairs, moving from room to room, I went through the whole apartment until I reached my bedroom. But I was hardly inside when my mother's voice was raised again in the garden. She was talking now to the cook, who was leaning from the kitchen window, opposite. When I had finished telephoning, my mother said to her, she was to ask me please to come down for a moment. And since the cook answered that I wasn't telephoning at all but, she thought, was in my room, Mamma, again raising her dramatic voice, began to call me. She repeated my name two or three times, lingering melodiously on the vowels. And between one call and the next, through the shutters, which were ajar, I could hear her grumbling.

I opened the shutters until I could just stick my head out.

"Here I am," I said.

"Would you be so kind, my dear sir, as to come here for a moment?" my mother asked. "Hurry now. Do as I say."

But she wasn't in the least irritated, quite the contrary, and not even impatient. Seated in a wicker chair at the edge of the circle of bluish shade that spread at the foot of the magnolia, surrounded by all her "sainted creatures," as she called them (Lulu, the fox terrier bitch, and the two smoke-colored Persian cats were asleep on the ground nearby, while Filomena, the tortoise with its humped yellow-and-black shell, was a bit farther on, scrambling over the dazzling white gravel), she looked up at me and smiled. She was embroidering: the hem of a sheet or a tablecloth. The needle glistened in her lap, while the garden, over which the July sun stood perpendicularly, blazed around her like a little jungle.

"I got all eights," I said, "except from la Krauss and Fabiani. Six in science, and six in mathematics and physics."

"My clever darling!" my mother exclaimed. "Papa will be so pleased. . . . Come down this minute and give me a little kiss."

She went on looking at me, prettily holding her head to one side, her lips forming her sweetest, most inviting smile. And as I stood there, unmoving, showing no sign of wanting to leave the window, she complained: "Well, do you think it's nice to make your mother plead for a kiss?"

A few moments before, crossing one of the living rooms, I had stopped briefly to examine an old photograph, in a silver frame, prominently displayed on a little table with other family photographs. It was of me and Mamma, in 1918, the last wartime summer. Mamma, thin as a girl, dressed in white, was kneeling beside me, against the luminous background of a garden (not this one, but the garden of my grandparents' house in the country, at Masi Torello, where, after Papa had left for the front, she and I had gone to stay); and as she passionately held me to her, she was turning toward the camera a joyous smile, absolutely happy, in contrast with the severe, frowning expression on my chubby little face, framed by long, lank hair, with bangs. The photograph, as I had always known, had been taken by my father during one of his short leaves from the front (it was his masterpiece, he used to say, and Mamma, each time he said it, nodded). But only a few moments before, in the living room, looking at it, I had understood the real meaning of that smile of Mamma's, married barely three years then: what it promised, what it offered, and *to whom*. . . .

I looked at her now, Mamma, no longer so young, no longer so girlish, and I felt my heart fill once again with disgust and bitterness. With the speed of film, through my mind flashed epic and melancholy visions of lonely, storm-lashed beaches, of lofty, inaccessible peaks, of virgin forests, deserts. . . . Oh, to go away, to flee! To see no one any more, and, especially, to be seen by no one!

"So," my mother insisted, "must I continue to stay here, sighing beneath your balcony, or does his lordship prefer for me to come up and woo him, in his room?"

No, no, I would go to her. We would talk. I would allow myself to be questioned until the moment when my father, coming home and seeing us from the end of the vestibule, would clap his hands to signal that he was home and was in a hurry to go to the table. What was so difficult about lying for half an hour? I would be very clever. All her attempts at sounding me out would prove useless.

And if she needed a kiss in order to believe I was

still a child, *her* child, she would have the kiss she wanted.

"No, wait," I answered. "I'll be right down."

And, with this, I drew back from the window.

XV

The ulcer had begun to fester secretly: slow, lazy, incurable. . . .

I expected no clarification from the immediate future; I neither expected nor hoped for any epilogue: not even as far as Luciano was concerned. But instead, at Cesenatico, only a month and a half later (I thought I wouldn't see him, Luciano, before school reopened, in October), there was, at least with him, a real epilogue. And how unforeseen and unforeseeable it was to the me of that period!

At that time I suffered from adolescent acne; and he turned up on the beach suddenly, one Sunday morning, when I had gone there very early, alone, after a sleepless night, spent pacing up and down the few square feet of my little bedroom.

It must have been about eight thirty. The vast beach was still deserted. Lying in a deck chair next to the closed umbrella, I had finally fallen asleep: a refreshing sleep but very light, since it allowed me to perceive the little sounds of the noisy beach day at its beginning—the bustle of the attendants, preparing tents and umbrellas, the cadenced cry of the fishermen pulling a net ashore. And there, as I drowsed, thinking that when it was ten or so I would go and visit, at their tent, some young people named Sassòli, from Bologna, and a little later would have a swim with them (there were five of these Sassòlis, all boys, rough, athletic, great football players and great swimmers: Sergio, the eldest, was actually training for the Scarioni Cup elimination trials, scheduled just after the mid-August holiday in the harbor channel at Rimini), all of a sudden I saw him in front of me.

He stood there, watching me wake up, his little body very white and bony, completely hairless, made even more frail by the enormous bulge of his sex which his gray trunks could barely cover. And he was smiling: a timid, shy, uncertain smile.

"When did you get here?" I said, without standing up.

A flash of joy and gratitude brightened his eyes. Then I wasn't going to drive him away! his look said. Then I would be kind again with him!

"Just half an hour ago," he answered, his jaw making its usual sideways shift.

"Where have you turned up from? Ferrara?"

"Yes."

"What time did you leave?"

"Oh, at the break of rosy-fingered dawn!" he laughed. "There was a milk train at three forty-five. Chug-chug-chug, it took almost four hours to go sixty-five miles. A record, don't you think?"

The train, he continued gaily, delighted that such a neutral topic had turned up, had stopped at absolutely every station along the line. It had made its first stop only ten minutes after leaving Ferrara: at Gaibanella. After

Gaibanella, it had come to a halt at Montesanto; and then, one after the other, at Portomaggiore, Argenta, San Biagio, Lavezzola, Voltana, Alfonsine ("birthplace of Vincenzo Monti"), at Glorie (Glorie! Had I ever heard of it, a metropolis of that name?), to "wind up" finally at Ravenna, two thirds of the way along, where, incidentally, it had decided to rest for "a good thirty-five minutes." After Ravenna . . .

I held up my hand to stop him. I asked: "How did you manage to find our villa?"

"I remembered the address," he answered. "Luckily"—and he winked—"for once my memory worked."

With that winning wink, he wasn't so much referring to our former intimacy as urging me to remain calm, not to grow angry since he hadn't the slightest intention of reproaching me for anything. Still, there was no doubt that he was reproaching me. Affectionately, but still reproaching.

"You must be hungry," I said. "Shall I get you something to eat?"

He answered, promptly, that there was no need. His nourishment, he told me—again pleased at being able to digress—had been taken care of by my mother, who, as soon as she saw him, was kind enough to put immediately in front of him a cup of milk and coffee "this big." He had eaten in the dining room with my brother and sister, who had got up just then. But since the two of them, as far as he could tell, wouldn't be coming to the beach before nine, and since he, instead, was anxious to see me, as soon as he had changed he had run off at once.

I asked him where he had changed.

"In your room," he answered, slightly alarmed. "Why? Your mother told me I could use it. . . ."

In the meanwhile he had sat down beside me, on the sand, so as we talked, our faces were mostly turned toward the sea. The water, out there, however, seemed almost invisible. It was one of those mornings, fairly frequent along the Adriatic, when sea and sky mingle to form a sole, pale mass, somewhere between milk and mother-of-pearl, and the boats, out at sea, seem suspended in midair.

"It's wonderful here," Luciano murmured at last, after a long silence.

He turned for a moment to look at me, perhaps to check my mood; then, very earnestly, he said he had come to Cesenatico for a specific reason: to speak to me. Recently, he didn't understand why, I had often treated him badly, and this after so many months when, on the contrary, I had been kind and affectionate toward him. And since his father had succeeded (his voice quavered) . . . yes, his father had finally succeeded in taking over a private practice, in Bologna, and within the month they would all leave Ferrara, and for good: for this reason, he felt it his duty to come and thank me one last time before changing cities, trying also to clear up all the misunderstandings that might perhaps have come between us. Well then: what had he done that had displeased me? He, to tell the truth . . . ahem . . . felt his conscience was absolutely clear. Still, even if I had believed any nasty talk about him, he was ready to give me, then and there, whatever explanations I might need.

I, too, at a certain point, cast a sidelong glance at

him. Sitting on the sand with his legs folded like an Indian's, his Adam's apple bobbing up and down, he spoke more than ever without looking at me. I listened to him. I listened to the hum of his voice in the vast, still air, I could even follow what he was saying. What had he said? That he was leaving Ferrara, that we wouldn't meet again. Good.

"So," he insisted, "may I ask what I did to you?"

"I thought I had already told you," I answered, calmly, "I have nothing against you."

He shook his head, sadly.

"That may be," he sighed. "But I feel you're hiding something from me . . . that you're not telling me the *whole* truth."

He remained silent for a while, pensive. Finally, after a cautious, sidelong glance, he asked me how I spent my days there at the sea, and if during that month or more some beautiful lady hadn't perhaps taken on the job of (he coughed, hesitating) . . . deflowering me. There must be a lot at Cesenatico, he exclaimed, a lot of beautiful ladies! Coming from the station to our house, he had already glimpsed quite a few "stunners" around, in the shaded streets, in spite of the early hour. And I (he hesitated again) . . . with my physique . . . would just have to look around for a moment, and I would surely have merely the problem of choosing. Women, on holiday, especially at the beach, think only of having a good time. It's simply a matter for those who have . . . for those who want to enjoy themselves with women . . . of knowing how to seize the time and place.

I had imagined that sooner or later he would come to his favorite topics (I had thought of that from the moment I had first seen him appear, through the fissure of my closed lids). Still, I hadn't foreseen the tone he would use: tentative, with no display of obscenity, curiously anxious.

I answered, in any case, calmly, that so far I hadn't met any married women, not of that sort; and this year, on the contrary, I ran around only with boys, mostly some brothers called Sassòli, from Bologna ("I've heard the name," Luciano intervened, at this point, nodding; "in my day, two of them were at the Galvani"), and that if I did encounter any woman, the pimples all over my face would surely prevent her from taking me into consideration.

He gave my face a rapid glance, and shook his head again.

"What an idea!" he cried, gaily. "You're very handsome, all the same."

His eyes ran down over my body, to the abdomen, and then he added: "What do you think?" He resumed, for a moment, his arrogant sneer of the old days. "Women won't make love with pimples?"

In any case, he continued, hesitating again, in the event that I . . . ahem . . . hadn't found anything better there at Cesenatico, I could always, if I wanted, call on him. He explained at once: a few mornings before, in Ferrara, as he was going along Via Colomba, "a well-built brunette," in her robe, was looking out of a second-floor window of the Pensione Mafarka, and she had greeted him with a big smile and a meaningful gesture. They hadn't said a word, actually, but he was certain: he would only have to turn up there one morning in long trousers (his mother was reluctant to buy them for him, but he would surely persuade her within the week), and, even better, in the company of a friend, and she, the brunette, would "entertain" them free. Now, if I was willing, that friend—he looked into my eyes—could be me.

"Can't you run up to Ferrara, with some kind of excuse?" he insisted, passionately. "You'll see: she'll not only let us come in, but she'll take us up to the room together."

Passionately: there was no other word.

I looked away. I raised my eyes. As it did every morning at that hour, a military hydroplane was flying along off the shore. The Savoia-Marchetti's silvery fuselage, distant, flashed in the sun. How many miles was it from shore? I wondered. At a rough guess, those four fishing boats out there, immobile on the horizon, must have it over their heads.

I stretched lazily, and yawned.

"No," I answered at last, coldly. "In the first place, I don't have long trousers either. And besides, I don't like the idea of a threesome. I'd never do it."

"You don't like a threesome," he stammered, still staring at me, his pale face as pale as a drowned man's. "But I . . ."

He said: "But I . . ." just like that, in a whisper, and added nothing else. He had begun looking at the sand, beyond the sharp points of his knees.

I, too, remained silent. Suddenly I stood up and said: "Shall we go for a row?"

He looked up, questioningly.

"Gladly," he answered, and was already rising to his feet. "But, mind you, I can't swim."

"Don't worry," I answered. "If necessary, I'll rescue you."

I rowed. When we were about a hundred yards from the shore, I glimpsed, standing at the entrance to the Adele Baths, my mother, in skirt and blouse, arriving from the house at that moment. Her right hand was holding Fanny's hand; with her left, upraised, she shielded her face from the sun. Not seeing me and Luciano under the umbrella, she had guessed at once that we were in the water, and she was trying to discover where we were.

"Oo-hoo!" I shouted.

I had let go of one oar, waving my arm above my head.

"Oo-hoo!" she called back. "Oo-hoo!"

"Who is it? Your mother?" Luciano asked, turning to look.

I didn't answer. I had resumed rowing with great energy, my eyes fixed on my mother, who, reassured, was already heading for our cabin. She was very tiny by now, I noticed; in a little while, when she came out of the cabin in her pretty blue wool Jantzen, she would be only a barely perceptible dot. From the water, we would no longer see her at all.

When we were about half a mile from the shore, I climbed onto the seat and dived headlong into the water. Alone, in the rolling, lurching boat, Luciano gave way for a moment to his instinct for self-preservation. He clung to the seat, as if he were afraid the boat would slip beneath him. Soon, however, he calmed down. In fact, as I swam around the boat, I realized he was following my movements in the water, he was admiring me.

"You looked like a motorboat," he said, in fact, as

147

soon as I climbed in again. "What's that stroke called?"

"The crawl?" I answered, gasping.

"What is it? Something from America?"

"From Hawaii."

"I'm telling you!" he cried, enthusiastically. "Last week, at the Docks, I went to watch a swimming meet. Nobody could swim like you . . . making all that foam with your feet. Is it hard to learn, this crawl?"

"No, not so hard. It's all in how you breathe. Every three kicks, you have to remember to raise your head. *Rum*-ti-tum, *rum*-ti-tum: it's a little difficult at the beginning, of course. Then, after a week or two of practice, you do it automatically."

"Who taught you?"

"One of the Sassòli boys. The eldest, Sergio."

"It may be easy," he sighed. "But I would never learn to swim like your bunch, not even in ten years."

Meanwhile I had started rowing again; but instead of heading for land, I went on farther out to sea.

"Well?" Luciano asked, in a melancholy voice. "Aren't we going to turn back?"

"With the sea as calm as this," I answered, "we might as well go out as far as the first fishing boats. Look over there," I continued, pointing with my chin toward two of the four boats I had seen from the shore, now less than a quarter of a mile away. "If we turn up when they're pulling in their nets, maybe they'll give us some fish, to make fish soup. . . . But apart from the soup, can't you see how beautiful it is?"

And it was beautiful, yes, after all. The sea so calm, so still (we seemed not to float on the water, but to fly, really, to glide slowly in the air), no matter how far I went back, in my memory, through past summers, I couldn't remember such a sea. The bottom, thirty feet beneath us, could still be made out: soft, marked with delicate ridges, like a palate. The shore, far away, with the blue mountains beyond, was now only a vague, hazy line.

Now it was at that distant shore, more distant all the time, that Luciano was looking. He had his back to me. Silent, closed in his thoughts, he seemed to have forgotten me completely.

I looked at him; and suddenly, there, in the motionless, burning air, I felt a strange shiver of cold. I didn't know quite what it was: I felt uneasy, as if abruptly cut off from something, and for this very reason, envious and base and petty. . . .

And what if, on the contrary, I had spoken to Luciano? I said to myself, staring, tempted, at that lonely back, like an Oriental ascetic's, which the sun was already turning pink over the shoulder blades—what if, accepting his invitation of a little while ago, on the beach, I were to make up my mind and curtly set myself and him face to face with the truth, the *whole* truth?

The offshore wind would begin to wrinkle the water in an hour, no sooner. If I wanted, there was enough time.

But, at that same moment when, looking at that wretched, naked back—suddenly pure, unreachable in its loneliness—I was giving in to these thoughts, something must already have been telling me that while he, Luciano Pulga, was surely able to look it in the face, the whole truth, I wasn't. Slow to understand, incapable of a single action or a single word, locked to my cowardice and my rancor, I remained the same little, helpless assassin as always. And as for the door behind which, once again, I was hiding (from him, Luciano, and from my mother as well), I would not find in myself, now or ever, the strength and the courage to fling it open.